WŌLVES LIE DREAMING

A.S. BERMAN

WOLVES LIE DREAMING

All rights reserved.
Copyright ©2022
by A.S. Berman
aaronsberman.com

DESIGN:
Pamela Norman
pnormandesigns.com

COVER PHOTO:
Ellen Carlson Hance
unsplash.com/@ellencarlsonhanse

BACK COVER PHOTO:
Frankie Lopez
unsplash.com/@stubborn5design

This book may not be reproduced in whole or in part, by mimeograph or any other means without permission.

ISBN: 979-8-218-08497-4

Published by
NIGHTWAVES PRESS
Printed in the United States

*For P, who knows
where the bodies
are buried.*

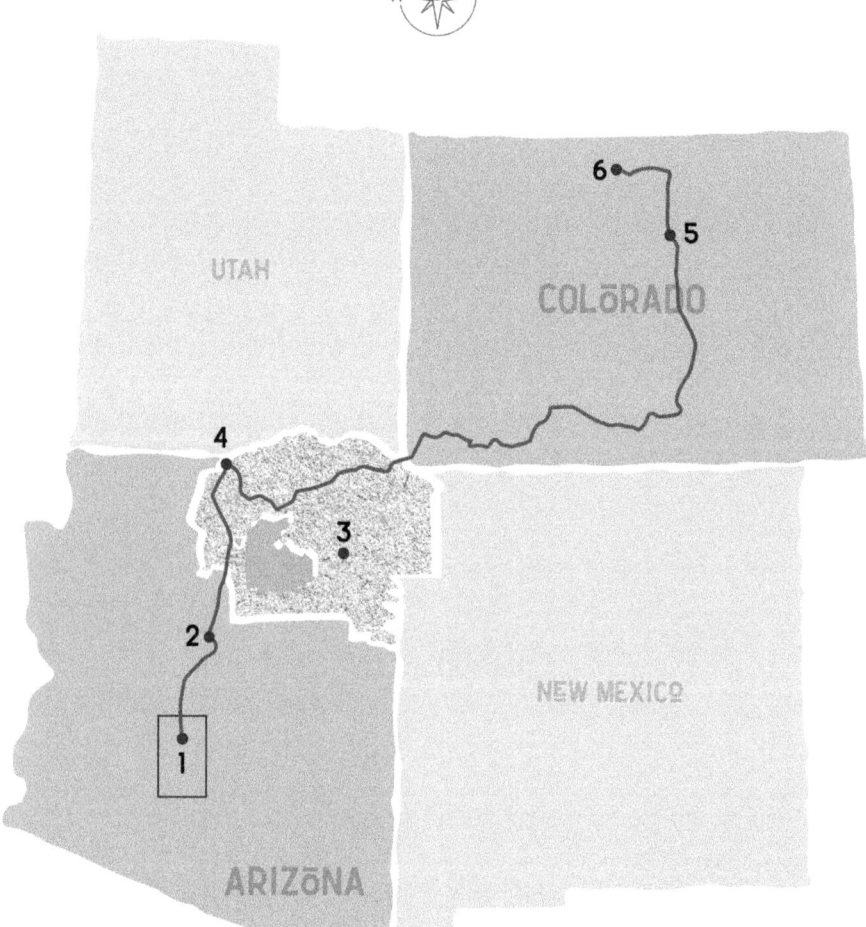

1. Phoenix
(detail opposite)
2. Sedona, AZ
3. Priest's domain
4. Page, AZ
5. Denver
6. Estes Park, CO

Navajo Nation

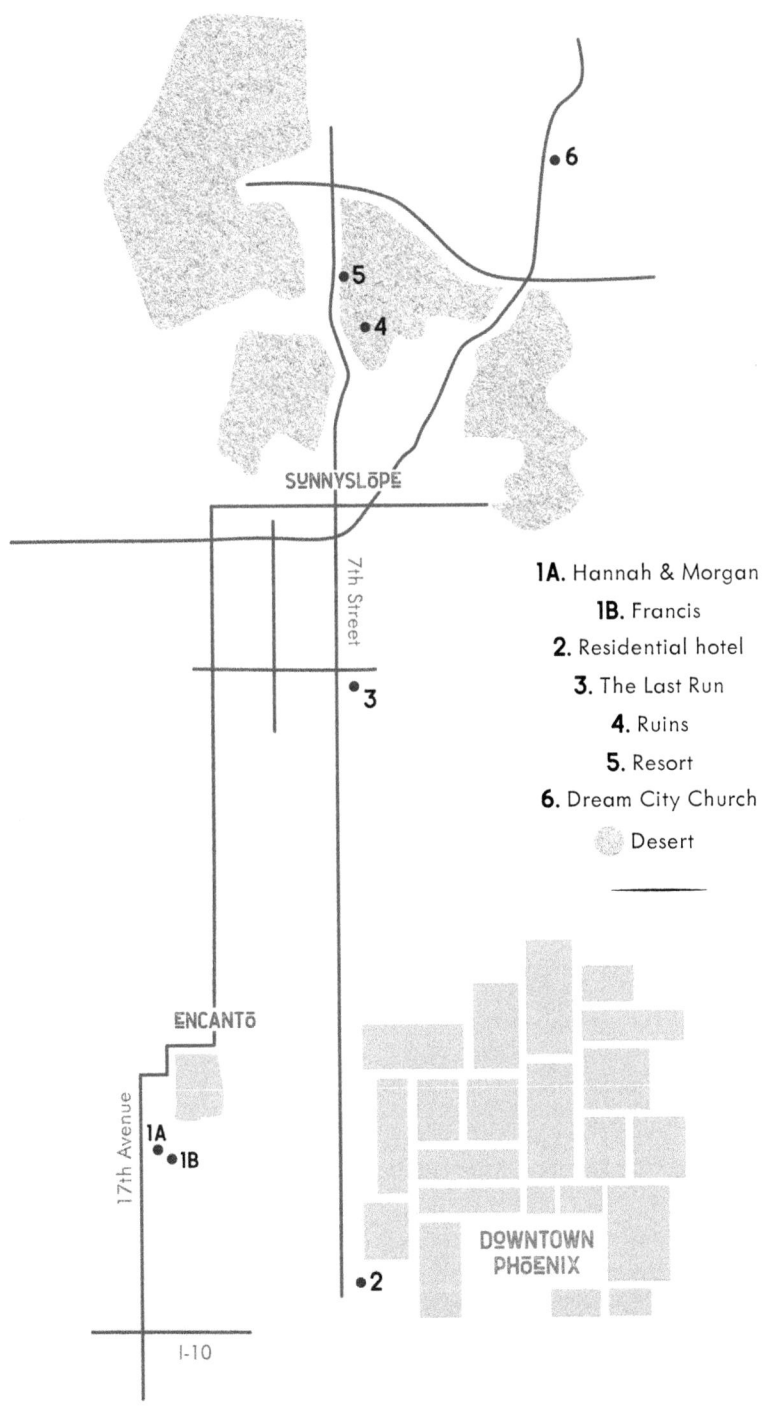

> *The comfort of conspiracy thinking lies in the notion that, no matter how chaotic the world around us may be, it is all in keeping with some great master plan. The most frightening prospect imaginable is that there is no hand on the wheel at all.*

SIMON BRADEN,
The Cold-Blooded Shadow

PROLOGUE
EMPTY VESSELS

Sedona, Arizona. It's late afternoon when the girls emerge from the forest. Some 20 feet above them on the bridge, two couples debate where they should have dinner, their eyes seldom leaving their phones. Further along the rusting expanse, college students take pictures of each other leaning back against the railing. Only a boy and a girl ditching their high school classes for the day seem to notice the new arrivals below.

Even from this distance they can make out that one of the girls has long frizzy red hair, which sticks to her face in clumps; the other appears Asian, peering up at them through black-framed glasses, a bloody scrape on one knee. Something small dangles against her chest glinting in the sunshine. Both stare back up at the boy and girl on the bridge with quiet resolve. If every day is the first day of the rest of your life, their expressions seem to say, every day is also the final, dying gasp of the one that came before.

Five hours earlier.

Trying on a small Thor's hammer necklace, Morgan swept up her long frizzy red hair and studied the effect in the mirror; she spotted Hannah in its reflection behind her.

Looking more like a little girl than the college sophomore she was, Morgan's new roommate, in a pink tee and dark blue shorts, was engaged in deep conversation with a tall, willowy blond girl on the other side of the crowded New Age shop.

'Maybe this is what she needed,' Morgan thought. 'Maybe sometimes you just need to be surrounded by patchouli and crystals and people who compliment you on the healthy color of your aura.'

Hannah had only just moved into Morgan's house back in Phoenix the month before after being tossed out of her old place for feeding the pigeons. Both had viewed this weekend road trip to the beautiful red mountains of Sedona as a way to get to know each other better outside the confines of their work life at Target, and to blow off a little steam between semesters at Arizona State University.

"Heyyy," Morgan trilled, joining Hannah and her new friend with a broad smile she did not feel. "Who's this?"

"I'm Erica," said the blonde, looking her up and down with eyes that weighed and dismissed her, "as in 'America.'"

"Erica's been telling me about the different uses of gems and crystals," Hannah explained, sliding her black-framed glasses up her tiny nose. "Very interesting."

Erica's gaze fell to the charm Morgan forgot she was still wearing; she made a face.

"No good?" Morgan asked, following her gaze.

"I like to keep an open mind about all life choices," Erica sniffed, "but it's a little too 'White Power' for these times, don't you think? I mean it's just so easy to send the wrong message today."

"Oh right, yeah." Morgan felt her cheeks burn. "It just looked kind of cool but yeah, I get it." Removing the pendant she hung it on the nearest peg, which also held an assortment of small velvet bags. Erica made another face; Morgan ignored her this time.

"I was going to ask you," Erica said, returning her attention to

Hannah, "what's that supposed to be?" She prodded the metal cylinder dangling against the girl's chest. "Is it...Eastern?"

Morgan concealed a chuckle at this clumsy reference to Hannah's Korean heritage beneath a feigned yawn.

"I don't know where it was made exactly," Hannah replied. "But it was used by the allies to send messages by pigeon during World War II."

"Ew, pigeons." Yet another face from Erica. "Rats with wings."

"Have you any idea how many soldiers' lives were saved by homing pigeons during the wars," Hannah asked, her normally soft tone cracking slightly.

"Oh my God, like the code-talkers," Erica blurted, as if this had been the topic of conversation all along. "I saw something on YouTube that showed how Native Americans helped pass secret messages around during the war and the Nazis never knew! Isn't that amazing?!"

Morgan was on the verge of pointing out just how little gratitude either the pigeons or the indigenous tribes had received for their wartime contributions when the shop door opened and a dozen or so people drifted inside in a cloud of white hair, pony tails and turquoise.

"Oh shit, it's almost time—nice meeting you," Erica said with little interest as she turned to leave. "I better grab a seat before they're all gone."

"What's going on," Morgan asked.

Erica regarded her with disbelief. "Simon Braden. He's reading from *The Cold-Blooded Shadow* in a few minutes. Isn't that why you're *here*?"

"We're just in town for the weekend," Hannah explained. "What's *The Cold-Blooded Shadow*?"

"I'm sorry," came a voice from behind them. "Did you just ask 'What's *The Cold-Blooded Shadow*?'"

A large, motherly woman with wild white hair and owl-like spectacles grabbed Hannah and Morgan by a hand each and tugged them gently past the still-growing crowd. "Excuse us, please—newbies coming through."

"We find ourselves in strange times," Simon Braden intoned in his polished West London accent, glancing briefly out over the throngs packed shoulder-to-shoulder in the back room of the store. "Chilled by the unshakable feeling that we are on a fast-moving Titanic, iceberg bound, with no sane hand on the wheel. But…"

Out came the handkerchief that made an appearance at every presentation he gave. Spying Lenora seated off to the side in the front row, he gave her a little smile.

"As I came to discover last year," he continued, "and indeed as I aim to share with you now in the pages of this new book, this view of our world is not quite accurate. It turns out that it isn't so much that there is no hand on the tiller, but rather several hands grabbing for it constantly, and all at once. The results…are all around us."

The leathery looking owner of the shop perked up at this, beamed at the author from beneath her mop of white hair, and materialized at his side.

"The original edition of *The Cold-Blooded Shadow* is probably known to a number of you already," she said with a knowing smile. "Before we go any farther, Simon, would you mind explaining to us what makes this one different?"

Glancing briefly at Lenora for reassurance he smiled, cleared his throat, and took another stab at explaining the project that had occupied the last year of his life.

"Yes, well, as Nancy intimates, *The Cold-Blooded Shadow* was originally published nearly 10 years ago and laid out my understanding at that time of the alien race that lives among us. Back then I referred to them as Reptilians—"

A hand shot up in the audience.

"A term, I hasten to add, that I replaced with 'The Others' in later books after discovering my fellow author, your own country's Howard

Mayvale, had adopted it for his own works."

The hand wavered momentarily, then sank.

"As I'm sure you can appreciate, I was forced to infer a great deal about these creatures' biology, motives and movements throughout our world based on various pieces of information I discovered in my research. That was until last year."

Glancing briefly at Lenora he continued. "It was at that point that I was presented with a most unusual copy of *The Cold-Blooded Shadow*. As I'm sure you've all learned by now, that copy, the only one in existence to the best of my knowledge, was very special in that it had been thoroughly annotated by hand."

"...by one of the very creatures that you had written about in that book," the shop owner announced with unrestrained excitement.

Despite this being common knowledge to those gathered—it had been made quite a lot of by the book's publisher during the launch of the new edition a month earlier—the audible gasps in the small room seemed to testify to the power of actually hearing this information spoken aloud.

"As you will discover in this new edition of the book, complete with that, uh, being's annotations, they do in fact refer to themselves as the Heliss," Simon explained. "And their internecine battles for power behind the scenes are the source of the chaos that so mystifies us in our own society today."

"So what did you make of it all," the shop owner asked Hannah and Morgan later as she finished ringing up the copy of *The Cold-Blooded Shadow* the girls had purchased between them.

"The whole space lizards wearing human skins thing? I don't know—to each their own, I guess," Morgan said diplomatically. "But who knows, right? After the last few years, I don't find anything unbelievable anymore." Hannah merely looked down at her sneakers.

"I think you two were probably the youngest people here."

Turning they were met with a warm smile from the attractive black woman who'd sat in the front row throughout the presentation. "Still in school," she asked.

"College," said Morgan. "Back in Phoenix."

Out came a slender, graceful hand. "I'm Lenora. I look after Simon when he's on the road."

Upon hearing his name, the author joined them, looking at Lenora as if for reassurance. It was clear to Morgan that there was more between them than just a professional relationship. But what did this thirtysomething, attractive woman see in the balding, slightly paunchy middle-aged man?

"It's OK," Lenora said with a laugh. "They're not stalkers. I don't believe they'd even heard of you until today."

"Well thank heaven for that," he sighed. "Of course if that's true, this all probably sounded like the most ridiculous nonsense to you both."

Morgan frowned. "So how would it work, these aliens wearing human skins? I mean that's what you're saying, right? All these important people are actually lizard things going around telling us what to do from behind human faces."

"I think you'll find all the hows and whys in the book, at least as far as I understand them. But yes, that's basically it." He chuckled. "It sounds quite mad when you say it out loud, doesn't it?"

A brief look passed between the author and Lenora. It reminded Morgan of those times when her father revealed "family business" in conversation, only to quickly glance over at her mother in apology.

Simon lowered his voice. "There was something that I didn't include in the book, mostly because I was still trying to understand it myself at the time."

"What was that," asked Hannah, suddenly interested.

"It's something I picked up from Br—the entity who marked up the book. I don't want to get into the specifics of our interactions but there was a certain sense I got from…it."

"A sense of what?" Morgan asked.

"Well, I suppose the sense of what a burden it all is, really. The great weight that comes with passing themselves off as human beings and functioning in our world. It drives some of them mad, apparently. Why there's this one fellow—one of their number, you understand—who actually prepared human skins so that they could be worn by the Heliss. He was one of several, actually—'tailors' they call them. Anyway, he fled the whole Heliss society, it seems. Just 'poof'—gone! No one knows why."

Lenora made a noise, shaking her head ever so slightly, and the author let the thought die quietly away. "Anyway," he said. "While there are a great many things going on behind the scenes with the Heliss, I am far more concerned by just how many 'empty' human beings there are walking about today. People filling our streets, rudderless, completely empty, careening through life, utterly oblivious to the damage they're doing to other people, the earth, and the very order of things."

"Simon, please," Lenora scolded gently, giving the girls an embarrassed smile. "You sound like an angry old hermit; what will you have them think of us?"

Morgan reassured them that they hadn't taken offense but Hannah remained silent. The man had, in just a few words, given voice to a stark dread that she'd felt growing inside her for years.

After parting ways with the couple, Hannah and Morgan drove around Sedona in search of a place to get some hiking in before dinner. Parking just off the main road they tore open a bag of trail mix and perched themselves on a large rock in a gravel parking lot across from a massive rusting bridge.

Hannah watched a middle-age couple survey the structure blankly as if attending the showing of a house neither was particularly interested in touring. "Empty human beings," she muttered.

A few minutes later she and Morgan scurried down a leafy incline until they reached the bottom beneath the bridge. There they discovered another world packed with lush green vegetation that seemed to envelop them in soothing mists, aromas and birdsong—the complete opposite of Phoenix's dry desert lands back home.

Stopping to rest on a small, grassy island ringed by a meandering stream, Hannah perched on the edge of a boulder, rubbing blood from a scraped knee. Smiling up into the leafy canopy, she said softly, "Do we really have to go back? I think this is the first time since I moved out here that I actually feel like I belong."

"Phoenix isn't so bad," Morgan said, taking a seat beside her. "Well sometimes it isn't, anyway."

Hannah played with her necklace, squinting against the sunlight reflected off the water beneath their feet.

"What Simon said back there; it's true, isn't it?"

Morgan laughed. "What, you believe in aliens now?"

"I don't know. It's not like it's the craziest thing I've ever heard. I mean my mom's always been super-religious, going on all the time about the Rapture."

"Ugh."

"I know. Still, there's this feeling I've had for a long time now when I look around at other people, the way they act. It's like maybe the Rapture already happened, and all that's left are these empty bodies walking around."

A lizard darted across the stream bank. Morgan's gaze followed until it disappeared into a thicket. "Astral corpses," she said absently.

"Astral what?"

"Corpses. Just something I found in one of those books at that New Agey place. Apparently it's this idea that when we die sometimes we leave these spirit 'shells' behind, and those are what people call ghosts. Or something. I don't know—I just skimmed it." She shrugged. "It made sense at the time."

Time passed. The sun disappeared behind the trees and the stream grew dark. "We should be getting back to the motel," Morgan sighed, hopping off the rock.

Reluctantly Hannah, too, dismounted, giving the vast wilderness one last look before joining her roommate on the trek back to the car. No words passed between them during their journey. A common feeling of loss seemed to rise from the ground and envelop them both.

Twenty minutes later they emerged from the forest, blinking into the last rays of sunlight as it poured over the rusty bridge above. The people upon it, most looking down at their phones, seemed as if they'd been preserved forever in amber. Shadows made melancholy by the emptiness of the vessels that cast them.

CHAPTER ONE

WHAT A FRIEND WE HAVE IN FRANCIS

Denver. Day's already lost the light, cold settlin' into people's bones for the night. Miserable little city full of bad roads and crumblin' warehouses, hipster types and homeless Charlies tryin' to eke out one more day. Cold's makin' my legs play up somethin' fierce. Gee-*zuss* I'm gettin' too old for this.

Could be worse, I suppose. Right now I find myself front row center in a quaint little church, all flickerin' candles and stained glass, warm and toasty like. Never ceases to amaze me how one of the Almighty's palaces looks like another inside. Like any good franchise, really.

Door opens, cold air on the back of my neck. Before she even enters the joint I smells her good and strong at the back of my throat. And I wonder: Is that the beast in me, or the man?

For what we are about to receive may we be truly thankful, oh Lord.

Outta the corner of my eye I see she's well put together. Not bad lookin' for a dame if that's yer thing. Short blond hair fussed over for hours by some fag hairdresser called 'enri or André or some such. A little more hippy than hip in them slacks. Then there's that nose, all pushed up like a sow's from nights spent peekin' at the neighbors, or jammed tight against endless dating profiles on the computer. *Don't worry, boys.*

I done squeezed out one pup years ago—I shan't be wantin' more.

Sittin' herself down on the bench a few feet aways, she closes her eyes and starts prayin'. I gives her a minute alone with her maker.

"Like flyin' coach class, innit?"

"I'm sorry?"

"These pews." I emphasize the lack of leg room by slappin' the hymn book rack in front of me. "Right down to the in-flight readin' material. Course what's the Bible if not a book of emergency instructions? I mean who actually reads the thing till the plane's goin' down? Then again the church turns that all on its head, don't it? A place of calm, safe as houses, while the rest of the world burns."

"How...poetic," she allows, before her head bows to the Holy Gee once more. I like it. Simple, direct: Fuck off, pal.

Not knowin' where else to look I peers up at our Lord 'N Savior hangin' there in that 'Don't mind me' way of his.

"Imagine it, Missus," I say. "There you are sufferin' something awful up there on the cross and what do people do? They march right into your house at all hours just to tell you about *their* problems. Does even one of 'em offer to help ya down, maybe hold a few drops of that wine to your lips to ease the pain? Like hell they do. It's all me, me, me."

She's starin' at me now. Then without a word she picks up her purse and starts to get up.

"Ya really don't want to do that, Mary."

Freezes like a rabbit, she does, that plump derrière of hers hoverin' above the pew.

"Did Matthew send you?"

Slickin' back what's left of my once magnificent mane I gives her the full benefit of my bought-and-paid-fors. "Name's Francis."

I can see them little connections bein' made behind those eyes as she takes in my grubby gray overcoat covered in stains, the beat-up old fedora in my lap. Am I one of Matthew's nasty friends is what she wants to ask but can't because our culture don't offer her an easy way into that question, least ways not this soon. We've only just met, after all. World's fallin' ta pieces all around us but there are still a few of us left that abide by the rules.

"Is Matthew all right?"

"Right as rain. Saw him just the other week as it happens. Good lad. Much to be proud of."

She plops back down on the bench again and I see it all dance like shadows in her eyes: hope and caution, faith and fear. And always, always that one reassuring hum at the back of the mind: *He's just an old man, he can't possibly hurt me.*

"Matthew's been missing for a month now," she whispers, leaning in close, anger bubbling up through her desperation. That her life's happiness could rest on the words of a crapped out old vagrant like myself—what is the world comin' to? "If you know *anything*—"

"Take it easy there, Mary. What say you and me take a little walk, give these other people a crack at Our Lord for a while?"

She starts to give me some lip but stops the moment I get up and hobble a step or two. Not so tough now, eh Mary? Can't quite bring yourself to yell at an old cripple.

With a little effort I limps my way toward the door; all an act of course. Give the crowd what they wants, I always say.

"Mr. Francis, I came here tonight because I received an email from my son earlier this week telling me that he wasn't coming home, but very much wanted me to come here and meet a friend of his. That he—you—would 'help me understand.' But if you're just going to play little games with me—"

"Life is a game," I says, a trifle louder than she's comfortable with. Her eyes dart around the church in search of eavesdroppers, perhaps, or maybe a little muscle in case the old man gets feisty. "Correction—Life is game." I likes the sound of that. "Hey, where you goin'?"

She's headed for the door and I'm getting that little flutter in the chest that always comes when the deer is ready to bolt.

"How can I be sure you even know Matthew?!"

"Ya said it yourself, ya got an email."

"Anyone can send an email."

"How's about this? He told me all about his mummy dearest who threw him into therapy every time she caught him dressin' up real purdy in her clothes. Ring some bells?"

That pretty little face goes all white. I gives her a toothy grin, push open the door to a cold night. Won't be sorry to see the back of this town. "After you," I coo.

Pulling her fur collar up around her ear holes she stumbles out into the night, looking confused, beaten. Easy.

Suddenly she turns on me. "Do you get some kind of sick thrill out of this?"

"Awww hell. I comes all this way to repair the gap between mother and son, my leg painin' me somethin' awful, and here you stand askin' me that?" I throws myself around like Hamlet with a case of the will-I-won'ts and grumble, "Why do I even bother?"

Outta the corner of my eye I sees her face soften a little and I know the bait's been took. "You will tell me about Matthew," she asks.

"Look, there's a little pizza joint just up the road. It's not much but we can get in outta the cold and have us a quiet little conflab without too many ears pryin'. What say?"

She don't say nothin' at all but steps carefully out onto the icy church steps, waitin' for me to lead the way.

Traffic's pretty light now. There are few people on the sidewalks, which makes me feel loads better. As I hobble my way over the ice I briefly wonder if there *is* a pizza place down the road. But of course there is. There always is.

"Please," she says, hovering at my shoulder, "tell me about Matthew."

"Happy to, Mary, happy to. It all started back in Phoenix…"

CHAPTER TWO

ST. FRANCIS, FRIEND TO ALL THE ANIMALS

See, I found this chick one night in a little Phoenix dive bar called The Last Run. Scrawny thing she was. Took one look at her and called her "Riga Sue" cause goddammit, I had to call her somethin', didn't I?

So anyways she walks in and I tells the greasy monkey behind the bar "Give her whatever she wants." All around me, the types you usually find in a bar sit huddled up tight, talkin' loud to be heard above the TV's blatherin'.

"Give *who* whatever she wants?" the barkeep grunts.

"Riga Sue over there." I waves a paw in the kid's direction. "Bottom shelf, top shelf, don't matter none to me. Ain't nothin' but skin and bones to her anyway; can't hold much. Fill 'er up, I say!"

"Whatcha want, sweetie?" he snorts, giving Sue his best button-loosening smile.

She looks at me, uneasy like. Them's the eyes of a woman wakin' from a Rohypnol snooze, having conducted a quick inventory only to find either her surroundings or her clothes ain't her own.

"I just came in to use the restroom," she says. It comes out all nervous like and I thinks, 'Aw shit, this ain't gonna end well.' Never let 'em smell the fear, kid; gets their Levi's twitchin' every time.

"Payin' customers only," the ape behind the bar says. He looks round the dive till he finds the appropriate sign, snapping a wet rag at it to underscore the holiness of this commandment.

"Just give 'er a beer, will ya?!" I snap. To her: "Ya drink, don't ya?"

"Not really."

Poor kid makes for the exit but only gets halfways before four more Cro-Mags, identically kitted out in Harley's best, block her way. You can almost see the brains workin' behind the beards, like the time between a scrap of meat hittin' the floor and the family hound twiggin' that there's a meal to be had.

"Saints preserve us," I whisper to the deer head above the bar.

By now the rest have moved in for the party, surroundin' Sue, and leaving yours truly outta the huddle.

"Where you going, honey," purrs a cloud of beard and B.O.

Another growls, "You can't leave now—the party's just getting started."

Outta the corner of my eye I sees the barkeep wringing his rag so tight the thing stands to attention like a prick.

"I'm sorry, I need to go home," she says, still clinging to the fantasy that her cooperation is in any way required. Not her fault, mind. After years of telling 'em they've got every right to live and do as they please, a few of the poor things actually believe it.

Don't get involved, I tells myself, finishing off my beer and pushin' a fistful of bills across the sticky counter. "This'll cover it," I shouts above the din. The barkeep looks my way long enough to register the dough with a curl of the lip before returning his attention to the scene brewin'.

Just make it to the door, Francis. Make it to the door and leave this sorry mess behind you.

"I'll be seein' ya, sister," I calls to Sue over the shoulder of one of the apes. "Next time, hit up a Mickey D's when ya wanna powder yer nose. Not a ounce of meat in them burgers but damn are they ever good about keepin' them toilets clean."

"Wait a sec!" one of the trogs shouts. "Wayne, don't you be letting that guy leave—he could call the fuckin' cops." Before I can make it to the door, two of Sue's admirers peel off from their tête-à-tête to block my way.

"Phone," says Wayne, holding out his beefy hand like an angry border guard.

"Sorry friend, fresh out, I'm afraid. But I'm sure the fellow behind the bar can hook you up."

But Wayne's having none of it. "Gimme your goddamn cellphone before I break your fuckin' arm!"

"Well it just so happens that I do have a phone on me somewheres," I tell him, rifling through the pockets of my suit jacket. Finally I produce the object in question and sets it down on the edge of the bar.

Pickin' it up with a smirk he hits the power button. Nothin'. Hits it again. Nothin'.

"You've let your battery die, old man," he says loud enough for everybody to hear, fishin' a round of laughter from his mates.

"Am I free ta go now, captain?"

Wayne laughs. "What's your name?"

"Francis. Like Francis of Assisi, friend to all the animals," I says, batting my eyelashes at him. "Bless."

A sudden violent shove sends me to the floor. "Whatareya a fuckin' faggot," he shouts. Silence falls over the bar, everyone movin' in to gets a better look.

Little Sue elbows her way through a forest of tattooed arms and sweaty leather, the bastards actually stepping out of her way so's she can better see what's happenin'.

Retrievin' my fedora from the floor, I dusts myself off and get to my feet—no easy trick at 71, mind. In the background, the television burbles on as I suppose it will until the last power station kicks it. Television and the cockroaches: the world's two great survivors.

"Barkeep, a pitcher of your cheapest ale, if ya please."

I slaps a fistful of bills on the bar, all eyes on yours truly.

The barman grabs the cash and goes about filling this new order, giving the others a quick glance to make sure there ain't no objections.

"The minute I saw all the leather in this joint I shoulda said to myself 'Francis, this place ain't for you.' I mean this fellah here's sportin' a vest with more tassels than a bondage queen. And his *muchacho*, well he's just a vision of loveliness in rivets and seams, ain't he? Sweatin' his balls off like no one's business, I'm sure. I mean how do you not know to leave the skins at home, man? It's 90 degrees in the shade! Surely the bad acne and neck hair is all the membership card ya need round here.

"All hard and desperate men, you are, but I don't see a single bruise, scratch or spot of motorcycle grease on any of ya. A little manicure here and there and any one of ya could be... lunch."

I thrust a digit at the mangy deer head above the bar. "*She* is the only one in this whole place I believe, and you've gone and ett most of her, goddammit!"

My eyes dart round the room. "Say, any of you boys gotta light?" My hands flutter up and down my suit till at last I finds what I'm looking for: a squat, antique lighter. "Well thank heaven fer that. Ferget my own head if it weren't stuck on."

Outta the corner of my eye I sees Sue and I thinks 'You simple, simple child—you could be well on your way to California by now.' But I get it. Hunger for closure is a powerful thing.

The pitcher of beer I ordered hits the bar with a thunk so loud half the room leaps outta their skins from the impact. "How many glasses," the barkeep asks.

"Why one fer every man jack in this joint!"

He snorts. "That's not gonna be more than a sip or two per guy."

"Well what the devil do they expect from the fellah they've just mopped the floor with?"

Laughter—the good manly kind. Any second now Wayne's gonna throw his sweaty, fat arm around my shoulders, pat me on the chest and say "This guy's all right."

But that only happens in the movies.

"Don't!" Sue screams.

Before anyone knows what's transpirin', Wayne's covered in beer and I've already coaxed a tall blue flame from the lighter. The fellah goes up like a Roman candle.

The gal weaves her way through the Neanderthals, hooking my arm with hers and yanking me out through the door so fast I don't even have time to drop the pitcher.

She bundles me into a red Mustang outside but I can still see them in there shouting, all those bulging forearms and green tattoos flailin' about like a fisherman's haul.

"It's a teachable lesson, Sue," I tells the gal as she lets me into her car, but stops myself from sayin' anything further. I get my first good sniff of her on the air now and suddenly I set to wonderin' if what's in her head might be a damn sight more valuable ta me than, well...

FRANCIS

CHAPTER THREE

'I GOTS ME A MAGIC PELT, LADY...'

Denver. Mary stops our little stroll with a hiss: "What the hell are you doing?!"

"I am *tryin'* ta relate a yarn, lady, if only some people'd let me get on with it."

"You're supposed to be telling me about Matthew, but all you've done is go on and on about some girl you met in a bar."

"Oh I see. Well I suppose Ol' Francis left out a key scrap of information. That Sue I've been 'goin' on and on about'—well she turned out to be your precious little boy, is all. Seems days or weeks afore we crossed paths, he exchanged his pee-shooter fer pigtails, if ya get my meanin'."

"You're telling me..."

"Matthew found hisself a priest on the edge of the desert, see, one that can works miracles apparently. Some real New Testament shit!"

"I don't understand."

"Don't you go botherin' yer pretty little head about it, Mary. Just as we don't bother ours about pronouns no more. He's a she and we's a we and oh the fun we'll have." I gives a little laugh. "It's the future, kid. Don't wanna get yourself on tha wrong side of history."

"I don't believe you." Turnin' she sorta shuffles off down the street toward an alley and I feels it then, somethin' that shoots right through me like the ringin' of a bell. We is nearin' the end of the line. I close the distance between us quick.

"Why send some old man to explain this? Why you?"

I shoves her hard into the alley, deep into the darkness. She falls on her ass, back against the wall, eyes wide, frost clinging to her fur collar.

"It's like this, Mary. Afore ol' Sue and me parted ways, she let on that you got yerself a fat little bank stash. Little slices o' plastic that can open doors fer the likes of me, one ATM at a time. And I need that dosh bad, sister, in the worst way."

"I don't understand," she gibbers. "Matthew sent me an email."

"Yeah well the thing about that," I tells her, producing a phone from my coat pocket. "You can sends those things from just about anywheres these days." I drop it in her lap. "S'OK. Sue's alive and well, fer the time bein' anyway."

"Matthew..."

"Jesus, Mary—you really don't listen, do you? Any idea just how hurt our Sue would be ta hear you callin' her by that name? And after all she's sacrificed, too."

"Please don't hurt him."

"Her, mother Mary, it's her now. But no, I ain't any intention of hurtin' our Sue. Well not much, anyroad. Bigger fish ta fry and all. Besides, how could I bring myself to hurt that sweet child? After all, she's the one what showed me the way outta this here funhouse. Ya don't eat a pig like that all at once!"

In the faint glow of a nearby street light I see her eyes narrow. "You're not human."

"No lady, it's a fact, my cuffs don't match my collar, as Sue once put it to me. I'm just an old wolf is all, fightin' fer breath beneath this man face. But that priest of hers is gonna fix all that."

"Money," she says. "You said you wanted bank cards." She glances at her purse. "Take them, take them all. PINs are all the same—5510—Matthew's birthday. Please just take them and go."

"Aww honey, ya know that isn't how this works." Bendin' down I brush her hair outta her eyes. Leanin' forward I let my suit jacket tent open like a college girl showin' off her good times. Her eyes go wide.

"Oh these?" I lets my eyes fall casual like over the two blades and their wolves-head handles peeking out from shoulder holsters beneath each arm. "Oh dontcha worry yerself none bout these. Like any man born wrong, I gots me some prosthetics is all. Course they do wonders fer a fellah's sense of confidence walkin' the streets alone at night. Fruits think twice bout tryin' ta squeeze yer lemons, if ya know what I mean."

"You're going to kill me..."

"T'ain't nothin' personal, ya understand. I'll be havin' yer bank cards, sure—I gots me a great need, as I said. But the wolf inside's got needs, too, and we only rubs along together so long as I stay outta his way, and he outta mine."

"There is no wolf," she chuckles dryly. "Just a sad little man that gets his kicks terrorizing women."

"Ya got it wrong; this ain't no two-bit hood yer talking to." I lowers my voice to a low rumble. "I gots me a magic pelt, lady, and you know where's I keep it?"

A flash of fear in her eyes.

"Inside," I breathe. "Alls I gotta do is reach down my throat...dig my fingers into that hot, wet fur...and gives it a good sharp tug till I turns myself in...side...out!"

At that all goes red, one blade plunging through the heart till it scrapes the wall behind her, the other longways across the throat, all at once.

"Mary Purgo! Mary Purgo! Mary Purgo," I screech through the spray of her life's blood. I wants desperately to lap it all up but I knows I can't. Born wrong is all.

"You and me we're gonna fix that, Mary." The lights in her eyes fade, fade, and are no more.

A minute spent wiping my face clean with a rag, another wipin' off my mitts and slippin' 'em into brown leather drivin' gloves. Rootin' through her bag I finds the wallet, makes sure what I'm lookin' fer is in there, and pocket the lot. Sort er out later; time ta blow this popsicle stand, and don't spare the horses, Jack.

Stumblin' outta the alley I sputter insults at invisible devils, occasionally hittin' up hipster types fer spare change. If anyone spies the blood on my dirty ol' raincoat they don't let on. Only folks more invisible than the old are homeless winos gabbin' ta themselves—double coupon day fer Ol' Francis.

Three blocks down I finds the red Mustang right where I left it, top up but ripped in places. Slidin' behind the wheel I try to ignore the flecks of dried blood on the tan interior, sloppiness and lack of follow-through being the twin privileges of the geriatric.

The harsh glow of the streetlights glints off the small gold compass dangling from the rearview mirror. The needle points West.

In His direction.

For only an instant my eyes fall on one of them campaign signs. And for just a moment I thinks of what coulda been if only I'd know'd the rules better at the beginnin' than at the end.

With a grunt I swings the car round across oncomin' traffic, squealin' off in the direction wherein the needle points.

Toward the wasteland. And the Priest.

CHAPTER FOUR

MI CASA, SUE CASA

Phoenix. A light burns in the window of the tiny guest cottage behind their house when Hannah parts the blinds early that Saturday morning.

"Francis is back," she informs Morgan, who's just shuffled into the kitchen half asleep in those horrible blue stripy pajamas of hers.

"Course he is. He always comes back. Just when I think he's moved out, I'll find the back gate open or cigarette butts on the patio. One time back when Althea was living here, she put a bike lock on the gate just to keep the meth heads out. So we get up the next morning—what do you think we find? The gate's just hanging there from the lock! Little fucker just pried it right off the hinges. I mean who does that?!"

Hannah, only half listening, stares out at the tiny house on the other side of the swimming pool the two dwellings share.

She's only been rooming with Morgan for about a month now, but already their mostly unseen neighbor has become a shadowy part of their daily routine. How many mornings has she peeked through the blinds before dawn only to find that crooked figure standing silently by the water's edge, the cherry glow of a lit cigar winking in and out like some all-seeing eye?

"Where do you think he goes," Hannah wonders aloud.

"Hell if I know. Few years ago I'd have guessed he was locked up in one of Sheriff Joe's tent city jails for DWI or something, but I don't think they have those anymore."

Sighing, Hannah opens the kitchen blinds just enough to let in the light.

"Morgan—there's some girl out back!"

Her roommate appears at her side once more, squinting through the blinds.

Sure enough, there she is: small, about 10 years older than them, shoulder-length dark hair tied back in a loose ponytail. An olive green Army surplus jacket hangs two sizes too big on her petite frame as she unlocks the door of Francis' place.

"Think she's like a live-in nurse or something," asks Hannah.

"More like some hand-jobber he found downtown." Throwing open the backdoor, Morgan strolls outside in her slippers and PJs. "Morning," she calls out to the new arrival, stumbling around the curve of the pool, still half asleep.

The stranger stops suddenly.

Hannah, still tying up her robe, rushes to join her roommate.

Trapped, the new girl turns, frightened blue eyes glittering back at them in the morning light.

"How's old Francis this morning," Morgan asks cheerfully.

"He's not here. I'm just...house sitting."

"That's cool. He off somewhere nice?"

"I...I really don't know. He just asked me to look after the place."

"Not a big sharer, is he?"

"You know him long," asks Hannah.

"Long enough," Sue replies, letting herself back inside the house and closing the door behind her without another word.

SUE

CHAPTER FIVE
TIME'S UNDERTOW

"What is this, Francis," I ask his living room, still processing my little run-in with the girls from the Big House. Cracking the nicotine-stained blinds I catch the Asian one looking back at me from their kitchen window. "Got your own little free range chicken run here?"

Switching on the light does little to banish the sepia gloom that hangs about the place. The stink of mustiness, sweat and cigars has a weight to it, pervading every inch of the house. And what a tiny place it is—more a large dollhouse than anything.

At the living room's center squats a brown easy chair facing the window, a green linen cloth draped over the head rest, fine white hairs undulating like sea anemone in some unfelt breeze.

Beside the seat, a small table offers up a full ashtray, some walnut shells, and three Marlboros in a lightly crumpled pack. Shoved up against the walls stand stacks of books, old magazines, piles of mail and large brown boxes collapsing beneath the weight of others. Absolutely everything here seems to groan beneath a lair of thick dust.

Terrible thing, time, comes the old man's croak at the back of my memory. *First 35 years or so, things take forever; nothin' moves fast enough. Then somewhere along the way ya hit the banana peel at the top of the stairs and whammo—down ya go like nobody's business at fantastic speed.*

This soliloquy bubbled up out of Francis shortly after our flight from The Last Run bar, in a drab little hotel room off the main drag.

Still hatted and coated, he'd collapsed on the sofa, cold eyes staring from behind those large, owl-like spectacles of his at something I couldn't see.

You're not even aware of it most of the time.

It had taken me a moment to work out he was looking at himself in the black glass of the big screen TV opposite.

It's the little things that remind you, the stealth inertia of life.

He picked up the TV remote, then set it down again.

The way ya put something down fer a minute, and five years go by and it's still there. Ya mean to move it, sure, but another three years roll on. And layer by layer it builds up around you: the Mesozoic, the Jurassic, TV Guides from 20 years ago...the hell 'n Havisham of life.

Now in his tiny house I find the little kitchen and start poking around inside the fridge, ravenous. I can't remember the last time food passed these lips.

I'm wracked by an overwhelming desire to drink in every detail of this new face. Pacing around the cramped first floor, I find nothing the least bit reflective, before charging up the steps to the second.

In the sliver of the upstairs bathroom I turn on the light and there, at last, is the woman of 30 or so I've only glimpsed a few times before, staring back at me from the mirrored medicine cabinet, open mouthed and breathless.

Fool, I think suddenly. *You just assume the old man is racing down the highway in the Priest's direction now, but suppose he isn't? Suppose, instead, he's on his way back here to put an end to the one person who knows what he's planning, knows the creature he's aiming to become?*

Though intending to leave this place, a weariness consumes me by the time I go back downstairs. There I collapse in the armchair as if someone's pulled my plug, the day's events rolling over me, pulling me under into dark oblivion.

CHAPTER SIX

CUFFS 'N COLLARS

The day before. Racing for the exit of The Last Run bar, I'm blinded by the afternoon sun the moment I throw open the door. From behind, a tremendous force plows into me and I think: 'That's it, it's all over!'

But it's not over. It's the old man. As he sort of pirouettes around me, he drags me after him down a few concrete steps to the parking lot. "Beat feet," he shrieks, a spidery arm jutting out to keep his fedora in place. "Which one of these wrecks is yours?"

I leap into the red Mustang convertible and fire it up, already throwing it into reverse when the old man tumbles in head first, nearly rolling over on top of me as we tear out of the lot with a screech.

The growl of motorcycles from behind cuts through me as we weave through the heavy afternoon traffic on a wave of car horns and squealing tires.

"Keep going straight up 7th," he shouts above the roar of traffic. "Faster, kiddo—don't spare the whip!"

On our left a mountain looms—doubtless why they call this area of Phoenix "Sunnyslope"—the guttural rumble of bikes close behind.

"We've got ourselves a bad case of the shitfucks, lady," the old man declares, glancing back at our pursuers. "Speed up but keep an eye skinned; we're gonna hang a right real soon."

When the right finally does come he shouts at me so suddenly I nearly flip the car over making the turn.

"You trying to get us killed?!" If he hears me he doesn't show it, but only continues feeding me instructions as we make our way through some sort of resort area, all golf carts and gardeners.

"Faster!"

I try to give it a little more gas without hitting people in the parking lot. "Christ, it's like Quantico," he grumbles to himself. "Up that hill. Come on, get the lead out, will ya."

The resort staff are giving us looks now. "I don't think we're supposed to—"

Any arguments I have are quashed the moment I hear the familiar rumble of motorcycles, closing in fast.

To my horror the twisting road grows steeper, the old man turned completely around in his seat now. I glance over at him just long enough to register the expression on his hawk-like face. Definitely not fear. Is it...elation?

Finally we level out at the top of our climb. "Park anywhere," he barks, "and put the top up." Without a word I follow him up the stairs of the nearest hotel block.

In a flash he swipes a key card through a room lock and disappears inside. "In or out," he growls. "I'm not havin' them orangutans discoverin' my bolt hole."

Not sure what else to do, I go inside.

I'll think back on this later and wonder why I didn't just leave the little hotel room, hop into the Mustang and peel off into the sunset once the bikers had gone.

"You sit tight," the old man tells me. "Watch a little TV, maybe, treat yourself to something from the mini-bar. I'm gonna have a word with my friend Eduardo—see if he can't sick security on them knuckle-draggers what followed us. Won't be a moment."

Now I'm alone. And right away I feel something's wrong.

The room stinks of rotting meat and sweat; cigars and fast-food wrappers cover the second bed, otherwise unused. A fat suitcase and black leather briefcase sit unopened in the closet. Above them hangs a fashionable suit too large for the shrunken little fossil staying here now. Checking the jacket pockets I find a crumpled receipt for this room in the name of Donald Agostino.

I head for the door.

"Whoah, whoah, whoah" Francis exclaims, bursting into the room. "Steady there, Sue. Where you off to?"

"I just wanted to get some stuff from the car."

"I wouldn't do that just yet, kiddo. Eduardo's getting security to do a sweep of the place now, if I'm understandin' his pidgin English rightly. Best keep out the way till they're done. Don't want them Hells Angels findin' you, do we?"

"Why'd you call me Sue?"

"Don't know really. Ya look like a Sue, I suppose. Now what say we order room service and watch the box, calm our nerves?"

The uneven smile he's been favoring me with since we got here falls like a soufflé. "There's somethin' off about you, Susie Q. 'Spose you tell Ol' Francis what it is."

I reply with a bravado I do not feel: "Something's pretty off about you, too."

"Is that a fact?"

"Yeah." I give him the once over before taking a good hard look around the room. "Your cuffs don't match your collar, Francis. At first I thought it was just that you're a little too scruffy for a place like this, but it's more than that." I stare hard into those cold eyes. "Behind that old-man face there's something else. Something dangerous."

To my astonishment he laughs, rich belly laughs. "Ya got balls, kid,

I'll give you that."

"Don't get me wrong, I appreciate what you did for me back there–"

"But this is the part where you say 'So long, Francis, we'll keep in touch,' that it?" He's eyeing me hard now. Then: "How's about we take a walk?"

As he opens the door I wonder if Donald Agostino accepted the same invitation. And where he is now.

As we make our way down the same great hill the Mustang climbed earlier, I realize that I'm not worrying about the bikers anymore, but the old man.

Since our arrival the resort has come alive with women in business suits and men in Polo shirts, the latter turning suddenly in mid-conversation to follow my progress. At first I think they're checking out the old man with his funny fedora, but quickly I feel their eyes running down the curve of my jeans. From the uniformed resort workers to the balding, jowly mess in the pricey blazer, I see them all out of the corner of my eye, their heads pivoting like clockwork in my direction. Fresh meat.

"What we need is a good stiff drink," says Francis, and so we duck into the resort bar. Snagging a small table by the window, we nurse a couple of beers, watching a parade of sweaty shorts march blithely on by.

"I gotta hand it to you, Susie Q," he says. "Your arrival in our grimy little berg has given this old feller a new lease on life."

"How so?"

"Because yer livin' proof that it can be done."

"That what can be done?"

"Well this, of course," he chuckles. "Ya used to be a fellah, didn't ya?"

I put my drink down.

"Why would you even ask such a thing?"

"Why? 'Cause you've gone and found a way to make yer cuffs match yer collar, as you so charmingly put it earlier—and I can't see the joins! Absolutely flawless."

"If I'm so fucking convincing then how is it you could tell?"

"Aw hell, at my age ya get a nose fer these kinds of things. For a start you don't walk like a broad."

"I walk like a guy—that's it?"

"Listen, pork chop, I'd love to chat all day but I gots things to do. So hows about you tell me how you made the switch?"

He pays for our drinks and heads out the door, leaving me behind to catch up.

Before I know what I'm doing I find myself telling him everything: about the compass and the land at the edge of the desert. And about the Priest.

If he takes any of it in, he doesn't let on. He just keeps walking, and I follow. "Where are we going," I ask finally.

"Left my wheels back at the bar; don't trust it being there after dark."

A sign we pass reads: *This way to hiking trails.*

We hang a left and I smell horses, summoning childhood memories of my grandparents' farm.

I turn to say something to the old man, only to discover he's little more than a silhouette on the other end of an 8-foot-tall corrugated pipe that runs beneath a city street.

"Well come on if yer comin'!" he shouts.

A pause. A choice. My choice. "No!"

"We're losin' the light and I don't fancy stumblin' round these parts in the dark, do you?"

I know what my mom would say, what I would've said even a few days ago. But so much has happened in such a short time, I push all of it aside, setting foot inside the tunnel before I've even made the decision to do it.

"That's it." The old man's croak echoes through the darkness.

But then the wind changes and his old man's coat falls open just enough for me to see, even at this great distance, something dangling from his belt on a long beaded chain. Many somethings. Credit cards, a dozen at least, strung together through holes punched in the corner of each.

Somewhere in this brain an ancient instinct puts two and two together and realizes what this means, pictures the dead fingers from which these bits of plastic have been pried.

I stumble backward into a sprint away from him, off into the cold afternoon sunshine.

CHAPTER SEVEN

CROSS PURPOSES

Phoenix. "Hey Sleeping Beauty, ya gonna help me unpack this morning or what?"

Morgan's words wake Hannah from her reverie. How long has she been standing here at the kitchen window, still in her bathrobe, peering at the tiny house out back? Again.

Morgan pokes her head out of her bedroom. "Althea's on her way. I thought we could all drive over to Ikea, but we gotta make some serious headway on your boxes first. After the first few weeks it was kind of cute, but we really have to get the living room back. What's in them, anyway?"

"Books, mostly."

"Speaking of books..." Morgan hands Hannah their copy of *The Cold-Blooded Shadow*. "This one's even more nuts than the guy who wrote it. Last night I read a few pages—crazy town!"

"You think it's all just made-up stuff?"

"Well, let's see. According to this there are alien reptiles who go around killing people and wearing their skins. Oh, and they're always fighting with each other when they're not doing awful things to us humans. So yeah, I thought it was pretty fucking nuts. Why, what did *you* think?"

Running a finger over the book's cover Hannah says, "I don't know. It sounds kind of nice, actually. I mean it sounds like they change who they are as easily as we change our clothes. How amazing would that be?"

"Maybe that's why the world is as fucked up as it is," Morgan mutters, helping Hannah unstack some of her boxes in the living room before dropping to her knees and opening one.

"Say...anything you wanna tell me, hon?"

"Tell you? Oh."

Morgan lifts a large wooden cross from the box, dozens of flooring nails pounded into every inch of its surface. "No offense or anything but I gotta say this is the angriest piece of art I've ever seen, and I helped put together a feminist collective's art show downtown last year."

"It was just a gift from my mom. I've been trying to figure out what to do with it."

"Your mom a bit...?"

"A bit. Ever since dad died she's been thumpin' the Bible pretty hard."

"And those nails, too, by the look of them." Morgan gives her a lopsided frown. "Sorry about your dad."

"It's OK. He's been gone almost 5 years now." She tests the sharpness of the nail heads with a finger. "Pretty scary, isn't it?"

"Oh yeah. Think she made it herself?"

"I don't think so. And I really don't wanna think about how much she must've paid for it, either."

Morgan holds it up against the wall opposite the door. "What do ya think?"

"What do I think about the first thing people see when they visit us being a giant cross that looks like it came out of a horror movie?"

"Hey, she wanted you to have it. And it'll make an awesome conversation piece." Morgan searches for a hammer and nails, which she finally discovers behind some water bottles in the pantry.

"That girl in Francis' house..." Hannah begins.

"Hell if I know." Appraising the cross' position on the wall, Morgan drives in a few nails upon which to rest it. "Niece?" *Pound.* "Sex worker?" *Whack.* "Who knows?"

Her phone rings. To show she's not the eavesdropping type, Hannah takes *The Cold-Blooded Shadow* into the kitchen, opens it at random, and begins to read a lengthy footnote at the bottom of the page:

"In the history of the Heliss race, a special contempt is reserved for the 'deus r'ghahl,' perhaps best translated as 'those who walked away.' These creatures, abhorring the interference of their kind in the affairs of man, abandoned their society to live out their days in remote corners of the earth. Of them all, the greatest disgust is reserved for Maldictus Karon. As one of only 20 or so Heliss skilled in the crafting of usable skins harvested from humans, Maldictus' loss is deemed particularly injurious in the eyes of the Heliss."

Looking up from the book, Hannah peers through the kitchen window at Francis' little house. "Deus r'ghahl." She mouths the words, struggling with their pronunciation. "Those who walk away."

"Hannah! Hannah where are you?!" Morgan bursts into the kitchen, her face paler than usual.

"What's wrong?"

"That was Althea..."

"She still coming?"

"Well yeah but she was just telling me about this virus thing."

"What virus thing?"

"That Chinese thing in the news. Trump was calling it a hoax the other day."

"So what's he saying now?"

"It's not him, it's scientists and people like that, people who know things. They're saying we should be wearing masks and stuff now.

Hospital masks! It's some really scary shit."

"Isn't Althea pre-med or something?"

"Yeah, that's why she called. She reads epidemiology books for fun, you know? According to her we better start making masks out of whatever we can find—like now. This is so fucked up…"

Hannah finds herself gazing out the kitchen window once more. "Think that girl knows about all this," she asks. "I mean do you think maybe we should tell her?"

"We just met her, Hannah," Morgan snaps. "You and me, we've gotta look out for ourselves! Especially now."

CHAPTER EIGHT

TRUCE AMONG THE RUINS

The Previous Day. Old Francis can smell fear on the wind the way most people smell rain. The aroma of the girl's fear comes on thick and fast like an ocean squall. The second Sue makes a break for it, I'm on her like the plague. My limbs pump stiffly, gravity sinkin' its teeth into my marrows.

Soon as she legs it on past the turning for the hotel I breathes easier. Susie Q can beat feet for Mexico City for all I care, just so long as she leaves me the nice set of wheels in the parking lot. That and the compass, of course.

Trees and bushes give way to desert scrubland now, stretching out for forever, it seems. The wolf in me relishes the chase, pulling this gray old man along for the ride.

Winded though I get, I notice something she likely don't twig to herself—that new bod of hers ain't doin' so good. Stumblin' here, stumblin' there, occasionally stoppin' to flop over, hands on knees, gulping down lungfuls of dust.

The distance between her and me shrivels till she stops, spins, and shrieks at me: "Why won't you leave me alone?!!"

"We are what we are," I tells her, feeling the twin blades shifting in their sheaths beneath my beat-up old jacket. "You know that as well as me, doncha?"

Again she breaks into a run, slower this time, like them bionic types on TV back in the day. It don't take me much to keep up with her now.

Hunks of life gone wrong sorta pop out at me from all sides as we jog on through the expanse—broken lawn furniture, abandoned duffel bags, parts of appliances, shoes, a sun-bleached car door with all its glass smashed out. My little hunt has turned into a cozy ramble through the great American subconscious.

"Where the fuck are we," I call after her. She stops runnin'.

Turning she struggles to get her breathin' down to normal again, then collapses into a laughing fit.

"What's so funny?!"

"Where the fuck are we," she mocks. "This is *your* town you psychotic old man!"

"What am I doin' out here, Sue? I mean how's all this gettin' me ta the next level?" Something dark crouches on the horizon a good 20 yards behind her. Turnin' she sees it too, and stumbles off in its direction. I follow.

Along the way we pass discarded shirts and shoes, thin jackets wrapped tightly around ocotillo branches, the detritus of lives lived in constant deprivation away from disapproving eyes. It's as if the long smugged-over rapture has already happened, the Great Beard in the Sky having overlooked the self-congratulatory in favor of those they've tutted over all these years. Of course it was them that got took bodily up into heaven. He told us it was gonna be them.

"What is it?" If she hears my question she don't let on. The shape on the horizon grows larger.

"Ruins," she calls back finally.

'Course we both known that's absurd. This here is America after all, we don't do "ruins." Closest we get is "Hey Marv, didn't that Circle K used to be a McDonald's?"

"Ruins of what?"

Slowly she paces around the area. "Old schoolhouse maybe? Homestead?" Her delicate little fingers brush the tall iron fence surrounding the crumbling stone and brick monstrosity, angry spear tips up top bowing outward in our direction. Fer all the good it's done; I counts seven bits of graffiti, at least.

She follows the fence 'round the wreckage till she's on the opposite side, peering back at me through the bars over a crumpled wall within. Around us there ain't nothin' but low mountains and desert.

"It's like it just sort of dropped outta the sky or something," she says.

Suddenly Ol' Francis suffers an attack of the guffaws.

"What?!"

"Whatdoyameanwhat? An angry fence wrapped around a crumblin' old house? Have you ever in yer life seen a better metaphor for this society – especially now?"

For a minute, alls we can hear is the whistlin' of the wind through the ruins.

"Look," I tells her. "Ol' Francis' got no beef with you. I'm gonna turn around now and go on back to the car; I gots ta see that priest of yours about a new skin. You don't try ta stop me and I'll leave you alone, capiche?"

Like a frightened squirrel she comes out from behind the ruins.

"Look here, sunshine. The seas are rising, the insane jesters are now running the show, and I'm an old man in a world past its sell-by date. All I wanna do is see out this life in the skin I was always meant to be in. You of all people should be able to understand that."

Rummaging around in my pockets I eventually find what I'm lookin' for, and hand the stuff to her.

"You'll find the address on my driver's license in the wallet. The front door sticks a bit but keep workin' the key and you'll be fine."

A cold silence falls between us before she finally stirs; her car keys land at my feet with a jangle.

"He'll want money," she says. "Twenty grand. You won't get anywhere near the Priest without it."

"Nothin' in this life comes cheap, darlin'." I tip my hat. "Thanks fer the heads-up. Oh and Sue?"

"Yeah?"

"Take care of my girls, will ya? I haven't known 'em long but it's a hard world out there; they can use some lookin' after."

Turnin' back for the hotel I feel on my back not just her eyes, but the cold steady gaze of the hawk and the rabbit, the coyote and the dove. And on the wind the defiant cries of Ozymandias emanating from the dust-filled throats of those who built what now lies in ruin: "Look on my Works, ye Mighty, and despair…"

CHAPTER NINE
THE NEEDLE POINTS WEST

Estes Park, Colorado. Before. The cloying scent of shampoo. Water creaking through pipes. Soft light falling from a bedside lamp. Another room in another hotel, 900 miles from Phoenix.

"How did we get so fucked up?!" The words are mine, originating, though they do from a different throat.

"We're not fucked up, Mattie." Clarissa strokes my hand softly. "We're just different, that's all. It's something we should...I don't know... celebrate!"

I *want* to celebrate; we came to the famous Stanley hotel to do nothing less. Yet I catch a glimpse of us in the mirrored closet door, huddled on the floor against the bed in matching white terrycloth robes, and feel my chest seize up with grief. Over the beauty of her. Over the ugly maleness of me. Over the valley that separates us even as we're jammed so tightly together.

I lay my head on her shoulder and she holds me, whispering: "We can *fix* this."

"You keep saying that."

"I know it's scary—believe me I was terrified. But I came through it on the other side stronger, better...*me*. I came through it as the girl you fell in love with."

"Did it…hurt?"

"There was pain. At least I think there was. I have trouble remembering that part now, to be honest. But I do remember the morning I woke up… as myself."

"Tell me," I say, curling up with her on the floor by the bed. She wraps her arms around me and I close my eyes.

"It was like nothing I've ever experienced before. So many sounds and smells. It was as if everything was new again. And my body…"

Looking up I find her staring off into the distance at something I can't see.

"It's like when you spend years stubbornly cramming your ass into jeans that are two sizes too small and someone finally hands you the right pair. For the first time in my life I didn't feel bound up, hemmed in, wrong. It was like I could finally let go and just get on with living my life." She looks down at me and smiles. "That's what I want for you." For a moment I try to picture her as once she was; instantly I feel my cheeks burn with this betrayal.

In all my life I don't think I've ever felt the full weight of my wrongness, my maleness, as I do now. Holding up my large hand I splay my fingers; she mirrors it with her own smaller one.

Suddenly I feel something small and cold thump against my bare chest between the folds of my open robe. Looking down I find a small gold pendant dangling from a long chain around her neck.

Following my gaze she smiles, turning it around so I can see: it's a tiny compass. "Isn't the needle supposed to point North," I ask.

"It points to *True* North," she replies softly, running a thumb over its face. "It shows you the path to follow to become who you were always meant to be."

Taking my hand she cups it gently around the pendant.

Instantly my body seizes up, wringing from me a sharp cry that echoes through the room. A harsh image burns itself into my brain: a long narrow road disappearing into a dark horizon.

The sensation ends as quickly as it began. I collapse into Clarissa's arms, heart racing. It's some time before I'm finally able to catch my breath again.

"It's OK." She strokes my hair. "The compass—it doesn't have that effect on everyone. What you felt, what you saw, it means that it belongs to *you* now. That you're already on the path to the edge of the desert. And the Priest."

My eyes are drawn to the television in the corner, which has been silently chugging out the same film the in-hotel TV channel plays all day every day. Jack Nicholson argues mutely with Grady in that impossibly red restroom.

"Do you think there are ghosts in this hotel?" I ask

For a moment she doesn't answer.

"I think we are all ghosts," she says finally. "I think we only truly come to life when we discover who we really are."

Laying there in her warm embrace, I examine the tiny gold compass dangling loosely now against my own bare chest.

The needle points West.

CHAPTER TEN

OUT, OUT BRIEF CANDLE

Phoenix. The moment Allison returns to the office from a late lunch that evening she senses something's off. Not a seat nor magazine is out of place, yet somehow she knows.

The old man is coming.

A desperate wind has begun blowing in from the East rattling the windows, bringing with it the choking dust that gives Phoenix's 4.6 million people the same dry cough.

"Dr. Pomerance?" She tries the door to his office. Locked. "Everything OK?"

It's nearly 5:15 and already getting dark; if the old man is coming, he'll arrive at sundown.

At last the door opens. And though a tad pale, perhaps, Dr. Pomerance looks down at her with a calm smile, shutting the door behind him.

"Everything's absolutely fine, my dear, nothing at all for you to worry about. And it looks like it's about time you left for the day. I hope you have a wonderful evening."

"I really wish you'd let me stay," she protests. "I could just sit and read in the copy room until the session's over. Or if not me I know I could get Rod to come over to hang out here."

"That's really very kind of you but it's completely unnecessary; you mustn't give it another thought." He gives her hand a gentle squeeze, edging her toward the door. "And I'm sure your boyfriend has better things to do than hang around for an hour." He favors her with a concerned, fatherly look. "Get him to take you for a meal, for heaven's sake. I believe many of the restaurants are open even during this virus nonsense, and you're nothing but skin and bones these days."

Searching his face one last time Allison finally relents with a defeated shrug and opens the door. "All right. But please, you know, be careful, OK?"

"I'm always careful, my dear." He gives her a reassuring little smile. "Now off with you. And do give Rod my best."

No sooner does he close the door than Pomerance slips the phone from his pocket and texts a quick excuse to his wife. She will no doubt sulk and sigh about the last-minute change of plans, but this is hardly the first time he's done this. Probably thinks he has a thing going with Allison. Let her.

A little insecurity is good for a marriage.

Again he opens the door to check—yes, only a faint glow over the mountains now. Has he left the rear door to his office unlocked? Yes, he's certain that he has.

Straightening his tie and muting his phone, Pomerance slips back inside his office once more.

Even before his eyes adjust to the darkness, the odor hits him, one that he hasn't smelled in many years. Blood. Lots of it.

"Evenin', doc."

Slowly Pomerance makes his way through the office, not so much as the glow of a headlight penetrating the thick blackout curtains he's so recently closed. Lights extinguished, the only illumination in the room now is a single white candle flickering at the far end of the room.

"Good evening, Francis."

From the darkness the faint yellow candlelight teases out a few sparse details from the new arrival's face; a wrinkled, waxy presence beneath his customary fedora. There the old man sits in Pomerance's own chair, no less—his usual perch during these meetings.

"Apologies for the short notice," he croaks in sepulchral tones that the psychologist has never quite gotten used to. "Couldn't be helped." A chuckle. "I'm afraid I didn't have time to wash up proper, neither. Came straight from..."

"Work?"

He can hear the man's lips draw back in a cool, wet smile.

'Damn him,' Pomerance thinks. 'We have rules about this sort of thing. An understanding...'

The fedora rotates now this way, now that, Pomerance catching the glint of the man's dirt-caked eyeglasses every now and again. "Got the room just the way *he* likes it. Very nice."

For the first time in the three years they have been meeting, the psychologist is afraid. *The way 'he' likes it?* A slip of the tongue, surely, but one that leads him to wonder who it is that is staring back at him now through the darkness.

"Puts me in mind of that scene in *Six Characters in Search of an Author*—you know the one I mean."

"Oh yes?"

"The father rearranges a bunch of hats and scarves on the stage to summon the clothing-shop manageress, expectin' she'll be 'attracted by the very articles of her trade.' Is that what all this is about," he asks. "A candle here, a curtain there, and I am summoned to this earthly plane?"

"Why are you here, Francis? Why did you arrange this meeting?"

Silence falls over the dark room, grown stuffy now for the closed door and windows. Pomerance jumps suddenly at the sound of something heavy landing on his desk with a thud, the violence of it causing the candle to flicker and smoke.

Squinting at the cause of the sound, he feels all breath escape him.

What rests on the desk before him is his own 300-page study of

Francis, its white cover caked with blood. There is only one spiral-bound copy of the work in existence—in his study at home. And now it is here.

"Not a big reader, myself, doc. But I knows bullshit when I sees it."

"Where did you get this," Pomerance demands. But of course he already knows the answer. He checks his phone. Still no reply from Helen.

"Suppose I should be flattered really," the old man says. "But I ain't."

The psychologist's eyes return to the cover of the manuscript, the streaks of red against the white paper.

"It's not just seein' one's own life boiled down into psychobabble that gets me."

"Francis...."

"What infuriates me, what seeps right down past the gray cells o' reason to the groundwater of my limbic rage, is this: Yer book tells me that the three years I've spent confidin' in you have been a waste of time. Ya haven't taken in a word I've said."

"Francis I need to know that my wife is all right."

"Ya know what's funny, doc? In all the years I've been comin' here, this is the first time you've ever expressed the slightest interest in those I meet during my hunt. Sure, there's been plenty of 'Why did you do this' and 'What were you thinking when you did that,' but never Word One about the poor sods themselves. Now why is that?"

Pomerance takes a deep breath, then: "What makes you think I haven't heard a word you've said?"

"Because once you sweep away all the $10 words and citations of 'other cases,' yer book sums me up as 'a man who thinks he is an animal.' *Your* words."

"Come on, Francis." He tries not to think of the blood, nor the unanswered text. Nor his patient's close proximity. "This is you and me here."

"But here's the thing, doc. I am not a man who thinks he is a wolf. I am a wolf trapped in a man's body. And every minute I spend inside it corrupts me. It makes me more like you."

So quickly does the psychologist lunge for his desk, he doesn't see the revolver in the old man's hand until his fingers are on the drawer knob.

"I'm a blade man, myself, as you know," the old man drawls. "I find handguns clumsy, artless, utterly lacking in intimacy. But I can slum it when circumstances demand."

"Why are you doing this? Why now?!"

"See I thought my time had come. Riotin' in the streets, Nazis in the White House, killer cops and killer storms competin' to outdo each other, all while our richest men squeeze the last few drops of blood from the earth. How's a fellow supposed ta compete with that?

"But I've looked into their eyes and I realize now that I was wrong. They're not beasts, doc, not like me. They've no passion for it, no souls. Just a buncha corpses flung about by winds they don't understand. This land is *not* my land, not anymore. I'm checkin' out, leavin' no forwardin' address. Gonna spend a few days just driftin' around the city, I think, and then pack it in fer good. See a priest about a spiritual matter. Thing is, I needs me some money for any of this to happen, you understand. Yer missus was obliging enough to hand over her cards and PIN numbers..."

Pulling himself to his feet, Francis approaches the man, gun still raised. "What I came here to tell you is this: Congratulations, doc, ya did it, you and your kind. Ya sent the last predator packing. 'Course I never said I was gonna go quietly."

The blade shoots into Pomerance's chest so quickly, he only becomes aware of it when he feels the sudden need to sit down. Francis eases him gently off the 12-inch blade and onto the floor.

"She didn't suffer," he whispers as the life pours out of the man, his eyes closing for the last time. "Much," he adds when he is sure Pomerance is no more. Cleaning the knife on a rag he returns it to its sheath, pockets the gun. And blows out the candle.

CHAPTER ELEVEN

SHE HAD ONE JOB TO DO

Phoenix. Behind the wheel of her little black Honda Civic, Hannah squints at people as they enter and leave the grocery store, as if the world isn't sliding irretrievably into madness.

"You can do this," she whispers to herself. Her gaze drops to the swatch of black fabric on the seat beside her, sweat beading at the corners of her lips in the April heat.

"Look it's as simple as life and death." That's what Althea told them when she arrived at their place a couple hours earlier. "Whatever anyone else tells ya, this is one contagious motherfucker, which means you've gotta protect yourself any way you can. And that means covering your face holes, ladies."

'This is ridiculous,' Hannah thinks now, picking up the mask by one of its long black ties. 'Everyone used to wear these things back home at the first cough or sniffle. Nothing's changed.'

But of course that isn't true—everything's changed. "Back home" was a Korean-American enclave in the suburbs of Washington DC where kimchi and specialty markets were nearly as plentiful as they were in Seoul.

"Why do I have to be the one who goes to the store?" she'd asked

Morgan, shortly after Althea arrived with two sewing machines and a plastic tub full of material.

By then the Target they both worked at had called to tell them not to bother showing up because they'd be needed to pull double shifts later in the week.

"Cause Althea and I both know how to work a sewing machine and you don't, and someone has to make these masks. Plus we've got no food in the house."

With a sigh, Hannah dons the mask in the car—the first Althea made back at their place—grabs her purse and heads for the store. In seconds her glasses fog up. "Why didn't I ever learn to sew," she mumbles.

She doesn't notice the two men coming up behind her until she spots their reflections scowling at her in the storefront windows.

"Look at that shit," one barks, the anger in his voice making her skin crawl. "Fuckin' chinks give us their disease and then they go around with masks to keep from catchin' it from *us*."

"Makes me sick," the other agrees.

Instinctively Hannah's gaze drops as the automatic doors open. *Just don't make eye contact. Get out your list, grab a cart and get it all done so you can go home.*

"Yo chinky," the first shouts, blocking her way with a massive gut barely contained by a sweaty gray tee. "Who the fuck you think you are, comin' in here and spreadin' your disease where we get our food?"

"I wanna see what's behind the mask," the other leers.

Hannah finds herself cornered between the pair and a display of muffins while shoppers walk blindly by. The men are so close now she can hear one wheezing slightly, the stink of heat and sweat penetrating her mask.

"I need to go," she says, still looking at the floor.

"Take off the fuckin' mask," the first growls.

Before she can react, the spindly fingers of the other reach for her face—and disappear as the man flies forward violently to land sprawled on the floor beside her. In his place, the new tenant of Francis' little house glances at her briefly before glowering at the man still standing. The shoppers who have, up till now, ignored them, are now gaping openly at the scene.

Pulling himself to his feet, Hannah's attacker manages to sputter "Fucking bitch" before Sue's fist connects with his jaw, slamming his head back into the automatic doors so fast they only open once he's slumped to the ground.

"Go," she hisses at them. The shove she delivers to the man still standing is so violent that he falls over his friend and into the parking lot outside.

When they finally regain their feet, they stumble off toward their truck, cursing loudly.

Only when Hannah has stopped shaking and allowed herself to be gently guided to a nearby seat outside the store, does she meet the woman's eyes with her own.

"Thank you," she manages, her words muffled by the mask.

"You all got some serious anger management issues out here, don't you?"

Hannah looks up to find Sue staring at her. "What's wrong," she asks nervously.

"What's with the mask?"

FRANCIS

CHAPTER TWELVE
ROADSIDE PŌWWOW

Navajo lands outside of Page, Arizona. Gathering yourself 20 thousand in cash is tiring work, especially when you're pryin' it loose from sticky dead fingers; Christ knows how anybody does it the respectable way.

My business wrapped up in Colorado and Phoenix, I gets my money all bundled up in one of them canvas grocery bags, and hit the highway for Injun country and the Priest.

First I twig somethin's up is at one of them roadside bazaars just outside the Rez—"Crazy Chief" this one calls itself on a large, hand-painted sign.

Stretchin' the legs I nose around tables upon tables of rugs and turquoise, arrowheads, feathers and beads, a few fat ol' wampums millin' about looking bored and resentful of the palefaces pokin' through their wares. In other words, yer basic American mercantile experience.

It's just me, the woo-woo types, and a coupla white families, their porky offspring rummaging around the tables, when one of them gas-electric sedans pulls off the highway in a cloud of dust. Out pops a couple, youngish lookin'. Each has a blue bandana wrapped 'round their faces, bandit like.

"The James Gang's found us at last," I squawk. The other two families look at me, then the couple, slack-jawed.

"Must be the dust," I says to nobody in particular. One of the men snorts, rolls his eyes.

"Not the dust?"

Another car rumbles off the highway and into the gravel clearing. Through the grimy windows I spy a coupla slant-eyes, each mouth a flat line of concern. When finally they emerge from the vehicle, each clutches a handful of Kleenex to their face.

"Chinks always go along with 'em," one of the men grumbles from beneath a scraggly red mustache.

"Go along with who? What is this, anyways?!"

"What, you don't know?" Red 'Tache's mate drawls at me with an amused smirk. "'Bout the virus?"

"What're you on about? Someone got the Hiv round these parts?"

A twentysomethin' Pocahontas with a long black pony tail grins at me from behind a table heaped with rugs. "Corona," she says.

"No thanks, I'm drivin'."

She guffaws at this as if it's the funniest thing she's ever heard.

"Whassofunny?"

"The China virus," Red 'Tache declares. "The Hong Kong Flu!"

"Sorry, friend, ya lost me."

Another of the meat kabobs proceeds to tell me that this flu was a) made by the Chinese and the Democrats to destabilize our beloved leader, and b) doesn't exist anyhow.

In the old days you'd get a leak of valuable information offa some TV in a shop window. Now I gather it all takes place on them phones everyone's got, leavin' folks like Ol' Francis to wander through the streets and byways of this land woefully unawares of the shifting tides a man.

"Plague, eh?" I strokes my chin thoughtfully. "Well I'd steer clear of the blankets here if I was you. Sounds ta me like these Tontos might be returning a very old favor, *kemosabe*."

One of the younger natives, a lanky young feller with a greasy black mane and a permanent squint, drops what he's doin' and spins round ta stare me down. Only the Injun girl's hand alightin' on his chest keeps him from leapin' over the table. She just drinks me in like something what's just fall'd outta the sky.

"Whatcha makin' eyes at me fer?"

"Just trying to work something out," she says.

"And what would that be?"

"Whether you're here for the River or the Priest."

Mention of the Priest stops me dead. Before I knows what's happening she has me by the elbow, steerin' me to a folding chair parked out back behind the enormous painted sign.

"WhatdoyouknowaboutthePriest?"

"Yeah," she says, "you don't look the River type. Too much fight left in you."

"Whata you on about?"

"Don't get me wrong; if I was in your shoes I'd be grabbing at anything I could find, too. Still..."

That does it. "Look, I can't spend all day jawing with the natives; I gots things to do, Jack."

I gets myself goin', comin' back around to find the two redneck couples arguin' with the "libtards" as they call 'em, the distance widening between them, closing, then widening again, each duckin' and weavin' out of the virus' way, I expect. The Orientals, bless 'em, are deep in conversation with one of the older Injun women, tryin' to make themselves understood through thick accents and fistfuls of tissue.

My companion clicks her tongue. "People looking for great spiritual lessons from people who have failed in every way that society measures," she concludes. "The Japanese are the worst. They come here claiming to be Ainu—their country's 'first people,' basically—and claim us as their blood brothers because of it."

"No good?"

"What's the point? We don't talk about the only thing worth talking about—mainly how the hell did we all get our asses handed to us by these Anglo inbreds?"

"What do they call you, sister?"

"Dotti."

"Unusual name for you lot, innit?"

"You know a lot of Indians?"

Touché.

Conscious of the hours of open road I have left between this shit hole and my destination I starts makin' my sayonaras, tippin' my tatty fedora in her direction. But something goes wrong and I crumble at her feet, catchin' stares from tomahawks and mouth-breathers alike.

"That's it, where's your ride," Dotti says, pullin' me up again and marchin' my crumpled frame to the side of the road. The moment she pins Sue's car, I can tell she's seen it before.

"You can't drive, old man," she says, "you can barely stand up."

"Looks like ya just seen a ghost. Friend of yours, was she?" I feel the wolf flexing his muscles in predatory anticipation; it's been days since I let him off the lead and he's got that gnawin' in his belly again.

But my words don't bring on the shiver I'm expecting, only a bolt of anger in those bottomless brown eyes of hers.

"You don't really get it, do you? How often this happens, how many of you 'seekers' there've been?" Her eyes narrow. "Just how not-special you really are."

CHAPTER THIRTEEN

A BRIEF STOP ON THE BRAMBLE PATH

For me and the girls in the Big House, the next few weeks flow into each other like a dream. Outside, the world goes quietly mad.

Any plans I once had of heading back to Colorado and Clarissa are subsumed now by that gut instinct every animal has during times of crisis: the urge to dive down the nearest bolt hole. Having lost my phone, I can't even call her, that number long since lost to memory.

Nights are the worst. Though I'm resigned to sleeping in the old man's bed, memories of what took place with the Priest out there on the edge of the desert, and all that I saw there, make losing consciousness difficult.

What was it I saw out there on the dark horizon? The crackling of distant flames? Tall, twisting shadows? Why are these things all I can remember now?

"That'll be the Lord Himself giving you a peek at the fate of your own immortal soul," I can hear my mother say. "You were on a path, Matthew. You were on a holy path..."

One littered with thorns and petals, mom, and my soul is sick to death of the journey.

In the bathroom, the previous tenant of this face looks back at me from the medicine cabinet mirror. "And what twisted past have you saddled me with, loveliness," I ask her.

Life grinds on.

With the pestilence spreading outside the cement walls that surround our grounds, the girls begin to open up to me, however reluctantly. I'm all they have now.

The morning after the grocery store incident, I open my door to find a purple cloth face mask dangling from the knob. From that moment on I seldom leave the tiny guest house without it.

"These people are so fucking reckless," Althea shouts one morning during one of her frequent visits, so loud that I can make out the words in my living room though she's in the kitchen of the Big House. It doesn't take me long to work out what has set her off.

Despite soaring infection rates, the people on our street are stopping to chat in booming voices that drop suddenly as they pass our yard. We are the oddballs on our block who wear masks, after all.

Lack of funds has become an issue. I entered this house about a month ago with $250 in cash, finding next to nothing in Francis' grubby old fridge. The kitchen cabinets yielded a half-empty bag of Bugles and a full sleeve of Saltines; the tap water is undrinkable.

Though I've been skimping as much as possible on food, I did have to lay out $40 for some of the basics: pots and pans, forks, spoons, plates.

The girls aren't doing much better. Hannah and Morgan's jobs at Target are in some kind of jeopardy from what I can piece together from overheard conversations. Althea is still managing to hold on to her part-time IT job for a local start-up but she's moved in with the girls to cut costs just the same. On hot summer nights we sit outside in our masks beside the pool, shouting to be heard through the fabric, until we give up and go inside.

"We got some mail of yours," Hannah volunteers one such evening, handing me a large parcel addressed simply to "Sue."

I thank her, wondering not only who the devil could know I'm here, but who but the girls would know I go by that name now. While they discuss the increasingly weird events they've witnessed on the streets of Phoenix, I open the package just enough to glimpse its contents: a few hundred spiral-bound pages. The title tells me all I need to know: *Adaptation: The Wolf Set Free.*

Sometime later, after the sun's gone down and the house lights dance on the surface of the pool, we retire to our separate homes: they to argue over whose turn it is to make dinner, and I to read about wolves and the human faces behind which they sometimes lurk.

CHAPTER FOURTEEN

LURCHING TŌWARD BETHLEHEM

The mud-spattered Range Rover eats up the miles, grinding up Rt. 12 toward the barren heart of the Navajo Nation. Two hours and change into their journey, Francis suddenly squawks above the roar of the wind: "I coulda made it on my own, ya know."

Dotti raises an eyebrow. "Way I remember it, you could barely stand much less get that beautiful car on the road."

"Lousy deal," he grumbles. "Of all the low-down toma-hooey swindles, this is the toma-hooeyist."

Catching the glint of the compass as it swings from the truck's rearview he scowls even more. It had all happened so fast back there, his little collapse by Crazy Chief's knickknack emporium, the young woman swooping in to his rescue.

"It's five hours by car, and not all of it's on a paved road," she'd informed him then. "Even with the compass I don't like your odds out here alone." It was only later that Francis had returned to that detail in his mind—how had she known about the compass?

"We still got a deal, old man," she shouts over the wind, "or are you one of them Indian givers I keep hearing about?"

"Course we gotta deal—I said as much, didn't I? But just you wait," he snorts. "One of these days you're gonna turn round and find yourself feeble 'n unsteady on yer pins." He sighs. "It sneaks up on ya. Like the White Man."

No matter how tough Francis talks, there's no getting around it—his rapidly declining health has been hamstringing him for years. Up to this point he's managed to push through it: the faintness of breath, the bouts of dizziness, the shooting pains through his arms and legs, eyes that mist over for no good reason.

And then they'd hit Sedona.

Surrounded by the city's towering red mountains, he'd pulled off the main drag yesterday for a burger and a pee, only to come face to face with his own mortality in the restroom. Washing his hands he'd suddenly felt one of his teeth loosen and part ways with his gums, just like that. It hit the sink in a stream of pink drool.

Now for the first time in his memory, the wolf inside him wasn't pacing around in keen anticipation of the next kill, but in eagerness to escape this man-shaped cage before the whole bloody shambles came down upon its snarling skull.

Francis has been through a lot in his 70-plus years, left parts of himself behind in different corners of the globe. He well remembers having to replace his top pair of front teeth years back when a convenience store clerk in Las Cruces landed a lucky blow in a dark parking lot. But this...

"Time, gentlemen, it's time," his body seems to shout. "Last call. Last call." The space where his bottom tooth used to be whistles, reminding him that Ol' Francis' Last Hunt is at hand.

Which is why he can't allow the sun to set on him too many more times between now and the moment he finally comes face to face with his salvation...and the Priest.

CHAPTER FIFTEEN

EPIPHANY IN THE FISHER-PRICE KINGDOM

***Excerpts from* Adaptation:** *The Wolf Set Free* by Dr. Lyle Pomerance. "...The subject in question—'Francis' is how he has always identified himself to me—came into my life in the fall of 2014 a piece at a time: a brief letter in the post, a hastily scrawled message on the back of an envelope tucked beneath the wiper blades of my car. He sought me out shortly after reading my most recent book, *Sadism and the Unconscious Mind*. 'Not to worry,' he told me. 'My sadism is purely of the conscious variety.'

"I should make it clear at the outset that Francis was explicit in his reasons for approaching me. He was not after treatment, neither did he hold out any expectations of a cure. 'I just need a fresh pair of ears on the situation,' is how he put it to me, and left it at that.

"Just as the professional law enforcement officer is besieged by those who confess to committing all manner of terrible crimes without ever having done the deed, the psychologist, too, fields his share of false confessions, particularly when he is the author of popular books on the subject of murder.

"I told Francis as much the first time we met outside a convenience store across from my practice. Without a moment's hesitation he described to me in detail a killing that had taken place in the Phoenix suburbs and suggested I check it out with the local police. Needless to say his facts were spot on; so much so that my inquiries aroused the suspicions of those same police.

"Soon, I began with him the first of what would become a series of semi-regular sessions after normal office hours. From the standpoint of the forensic psychologist, the appeal of these interviews was overwhelming. Here was the opportunity to observe the human predator 'in the wild,' without influence of fear nor favor that incarceration can bring. He had but one condition: 'Don't write about anything I tell you until Ol' Francis has breathed his last...'

"...which is when Francis told me 'I haven't always been like this, you know. I wasn't one of these creased cranium types, torturin' the family canary while still in rompers.'

"According to Francis, he had lived a quiet, ordinary life until a stroke landed him in the hospital several years ago. While convalescing in a rehabilitation clinic, his worldview began to change.

"'They had this little basement, doc,' he told me. 'Every morning some glandular case in blue scrubs would take me down in the elevator where they had themselves this little Fisher-Price town: all AstroTurf and plastic houses. But then, just to fuck with you, I suppose, they had this real car parked in there, too.

"'Well there was no way in hell anyone was gonna let me behind the wheel anytime soon, so instead we went into this tiny plastic store. Empty cereal boxes on red and blue plastic shelves, and this ridiculous plastic shopping cart—my God the tremors it set off in my brain.'

"These 'tremors,' it transpired, were not ones of the flesh but rather of the mind. 'For years and years I'd been struggling,' he explained. 'Wrestling with this maddening disconnect between the people I saw with my eyes and the feelin' that each and every one of them was hollow—they didn't exist; I was trudging around a world full of decoys.' The model city had given my patient a model for understanding what he saw when he looked at you and me.

"A few days into his stay at the rehab center, one of his carers was found dead in the basement, his head slammed in the door of the automobile in that ersatz town. It was some weeks before Francis was finally discharged from that facility. Suspicion, it seems, never fell on him.

"It was shortly after he told me this story that he first mentioned the wolf. 'Like most of the animal kingdom, mankind has been a real shit to the wolf,' Francis said. 'Hunted them to near extinction in some places. Yet every now and then we reintroduce them back into the wild.'

"'I'm not sure I follow,' I told him. I can still remember the look of exasperation and pity he gave me then.

"'The point isn't that men nearly wiped the predators off the face of the earth, but that the wolf is able to manipulate them into protecting him. Just long enough for him to get his numbers up and his fangs into the next fellow that comes along.'"

FRANCIS

CHAPTER SIXTEEN
END OF THE LINE

Injun lands whip by us at a peppy clip, squaw at the wheel makin' good time. "Fancy bein' my getaway moll, little lady?"

She gives me a blink-n-you'd-miss-it smile.

"What's gonna happen to my car back there, anyways," I ask.

"It's not your car."

"Aha! So ya *did* recognize it after all! Out with it, kiddo."

Another grin, but Ol' Francis still ain't gettin' his questions answered. A dilapidated shack whizzes by, little more 'n a few bits of plywood, really. No poverty more beautiful than reservation poverty.

"So you met my Sue then? The skirt who drove that car, I mean."

Another quick glance in my direction, furrowed brows this time.

"Course she might've been Matthew then. Never got ta meet the fruit myself but I imagine I knows the type." I give her the universal limp wrist sign case she's a touch slow. "You gots shirt-lifters round these parts?"

"Anyone ever tell you you talk too much?"

"Merely passin' the time is all."

We rush past another little ruin, plywood punctuation amongst the long miles of crops and dust. "Still, I've gots me a theory about the queerdos and ladymen. Downright scientific, too."

Pocahontas begs me to share by ignoring me completely.

"Happens all the time in nature—an animal flips the restroom sign dependin' on what other animals in the area need, ya see? Lady clownfish queen bites the dust and one of her alpha males says 'Don't mind me lads' and becomes a lady hisself to fill the gap. God's honest truth! Certain kinds of eel, coral, I know there are some other examples, too—saw it on them nature shows. Same happens with our species, don't it? I mean you ever met Queer One that don't have a story about bein' groped up at the age of 4 by his Uncle Bill or the neighbor or the good reverend after choir? Clownfish all of 'em."

"What kind of bullshit is this?"

"Well it's simple, innit? There you are, a little lad of 5 or 6 mindin' yer own business, and some fruit comes along and sticks his pecker in yer face. Poof, yer brain gets the signal—'A woman is needed here and now—stat!' So that brain rewires itself as a ladyman. Sci-en-tif-ic!"

Afore I knows what's happenin' she swerves us clear off the road and into a gravel trap, pickup comin' to rest just a few yards from another one of them wooden shacks.

"Jesus Christ, woman—ya tryin' to croak me?!"

The engine's idlin' rough, crops rustlin' all round, and she just stares me down like teachers did back in my day afore kids was packin' heat.

"You're not ready," she says.

"What are you on about? Not ready for what?"

"All this talk, talk, talk, talk about nothing, this trying to be 'a character.' You're scared, old man. Scared of what's waiting for you in the desert once we get where we're going." She lets the dangling compass rest in her palm for a moment afore she bats it away. "You're not ready for the Priest."

"But Sue or Matthew or whoever the fuck was, that it?"

"Your friend was running toward something. That kind of

commitment gives you the inner strength you need to survive. You? You're running away from a feeble body, failing eyes...the end that waits for you just around the corner. God only knows what the Priest would make of you. There probably wouldn't be enough left to bury."

"So that's the way ya see me, eh?" I nod at the derelict shack beside us. "One more clapped out abode waitin' ta be steamrolled into tomorrow?"

She laughs. "You look around and see the empty land and rusted-out trucks and cows roaming free and think 'These savages aren't fit for anything but drinking themselves blind and selling jewelry by the side of the road. We let them live out here for free and they can't even be bothered to keep their houses from falling down.'"

"Ha! Look who's lecturin' me about perceptions, sister. 'He's an old man, got no stayin' power, might just as well shuffle off into the abyss and make room for perky-titted pups like me.' Well don't you go worryin' yer pretty little headdress about me. Ain't no priest gonna get the best of Ol' Francis."

"What your Sue sought was only a change that would speed her on her way to greater self-enlightenment, a nudge along a path she'd been walking all her life. But you, Francis...What you're chasing is raw power. And that's why you'll fail. It will eat you alive."

Still, at long last Pocahontas gets us back on the road again and I'm dumb to our surroundings till we come to a stop yet again.

"This is it," she says, nodding at the open desert. "Keep walking in that direction and you'll find what you're after."

"End of the line, Francis," I tells myself, sliding out of the pickup. But I could be a coyote fart three counties back fer all the attention she pays me now. Slingin' the bag over my shoulder I gives her the old vulpine stare. When she does finally look my way that purdy little face of hers is all business.

Before I can grab the tiny compass dangling from the rearview, she plucks it herself, dropping the sucker into the armrest compartment, just like that. For a split second I see a whole lot more of them squirreled away in there, too.

"Suppose you tells me how many times you've made this little drop-off, sister."

"It'll be getting dark soon and you wanna be there by the time it does. You've got a good half-hour hike ahead of you. Maybe more, you being so old."

Them eyes of hers finally settle on me and whatever itch I've got to punch her dance card then and there disappears. That's 'cause looking back at me is something older than the tooth-like mountains and mesas that crowd us now.

"Don't you be pullin' none of that Injun shit on me, sunshine. Don't you people get the ice shits over skinwalkers and the like?"

"Our beliefs are a lot like those crumbling houses back there. We keep them around so long as they're useful, before letting them tip back into the dust. Like our elders."

SUE

CHAPTER SEVENTEEN

21ST CENTURY COMMUNICATION BLUES

It takes me two full days to read the complete manuscript of *Adaptation: The Wolf Set Free*; another two to recover. And all I can think is 'I've just handed humanity over to…this?' What new hell will Francis bring down upon countless innocent people once his nature is given the teeth and claws he craves? Has the Priest already granted him his wish? Is the wolf on his way back here now to finish me off?

I stop leaving the house during the day. Late at night I skim the leaves from our little pool long after the last light in the Big House has gone out, gazing up at the stars as the water tugs gently at the skimmer. After going to hell and back for this new skin, it seems I now spend my nights trying to leave it behind for longer and longer periods of time.

I've put it off long enough, I decide on one such evening; I need to talk to Clarissa but I have no idea what her number is. I haven't dialed it since punching it into my phone years ago, and that phone disappeared somewhere between here and Colorado.

Not knowing what else to do, I ask Hannah for advice. Disappearing into her room for a moment she returns with a laptop.

"What's her full name?"

I give it to her. The moment she opens up Twitter I feel like a complete idiot.

"This her?"

It is. "But I'm locked out of everything," I explain. "Twitter, email—my whole life was on the phone I lost."

Hannah thinks for a moment, then asks for my burner phone number, which she proceeds to leave in a comment on Clarissa's latest post, saying "My friend Sue wants to get in touch but forgot your number."

"Not 'Sue,'" I snap. "Sorry, it's just she's only ever known me...as Matthew."

Hannah's eyes widen over her face mask for a moment. Then she changes the name on the screen to "Matthew" before clicking Send.

CHAPTER EIGHTEEN

SUBMISSION

The sun beats down on the old man. Though he totters clumsily over loose rocks and perilous cracks in the sunbaked earth, he never falters, nor does he experience the slightest doubt that he shall find what he has come all this way for. He's an hour and 10 minutes into his journey, his water bottle long since emptied, when he rounds a great low mountain. The valley opens wide before him.

Even before he can make out the tents on the horizon, he sees wisps of white smoke emanating from something atop a distant mesa.

"Hot damn," he croaks between dry, cracked lips. A terrible wind kicks up suddenly, blanketing the area in thick clouds of dust.

Francis does not recognize the 12 for what they are until he's but a few yards from the closest of their number. In a land strewn with rocks large and small, they seem only boulders at first—boulders someone has gone to a great deal of trouble to arrange in a row some 10 feet apart, stretching from left to right before him like supermarket bollards.

It is the fingers he makes out first.

With a thud his bag hits the earth, another tooth making good its escape from between parched lips.

At once he's overcome with the knowledge that it would be as pointless to unsheathe his knives here as it would be to retrace his steps back to the dead roads that brought him here.

Carefully, he studies the figures as he approaches them.

Nine men, three women; he can see that now. All stripped to the waist, kneeling in his direction, asses raised to the sky like macabre sundials. Their spindly arms are trussed up tightly behind their backs, broken fingers bristling like sea anemone in the hot breath of this dry Sargasso Sea. Bare backs, purpled and caramelized in the desert sun, heads buried up to their shoulders in the scorched earth.

Submission.

CHAPTER NINETEEN

IN THE SUN, THE CITY LIES DREAMING

The following afternoon I'm perched on the side of a mountain when my phone rings. Below, traffic has ground to a trickle as the president's motorcade arrives at the intriguingly named Dream City Church. In the past few weeks this mountain has become the destination of my morning amble; that *he* would defile my only refuge with his presence, and do so solely to address his disciples, feels both a violation and providence.

Answering the phone I wonder what the range of an RPG might be, and if its use would make the slightest difference to our nation's downward trajectory.

"Matthew? I'm sorry...Sue, is that you?"

Leaping to my feet I pace so fast I nearly slip on a fairy ring of used syringes. Down below, undulating lines of red hats and American flags flank the presidential route as a seam of darkness thickens between them: the unmistakable carapace of armored police.

"You sound so different," Clarissa crackles over the poor connection. Excited and apprehensive, certainly, but her voice is also shot through with a vein of something else. "How are you ... adjusting?"

"It's a lot to wrap my head around," I confess. "Well you know what that's like."

The music of her laughter fills my ear, yet this gaiety leaves as quickly as it appears. I know what she's about to tell me.

"Matthew, your mother. Have you heard?"

"She's dead." It's neither a question nor a statement, more a remembering of something I feel I've always known. "How?"

"All I know is what's been online. I'm so sorry—"

"How?!" My voice reverberates through the valley, across the highway to the Dream City Church.

The silence that follows tells me everything she apparently cannot. Nobody hesitates to relate an instance of shooting or vehicular misadventure. Between television and our own daily observations, we more or less expect one of these will befall us all sooner or later.

"She was cut up," I venture aloud.

"Yes," Clarissa admits. "They think it was robbery—her bank account was drained. Whoever did it hit ATMs all over town afterward."

"How else does a man get his hand on 20 grand," I wonder aloud. "I gotta go."

"But Matthew...!"

Terminating the call, I feel a darkness welling up inside me despite the sun's glare. Across the wide expanse, the faithful welcome the ass into their ersatz Jerusalem, no longer insisting that it bear into their midst a Holy King.

CHAPTER TWENTY

EYES WIDE SHUT

The skin on the back of the old man's neck crawls.

The figure approaching him seems to glide, feet concealed by long brown robes stained white with dust. Staring out at him from between the folds of a cowl, a ceramic face like that of a Roman alabaster statue, its pupil-less eyes the same fired clay that makes up the rest of its features. Only a dab of crimson at the temples hints at the silk ribbons holding the expressionless visage in place.

"Takin' this virus hooey awful serious, ain't ya," the old man says with a chuckle. But the silent acolyte only turns and glides back across the rocks to a large tent of animal hides and Native American patterned blankets that Francis hadn't noticed till this moment. Smaller teepees in the distance undulate slightly in some unfelt breeze.

The instant Francis passes between two of the bodies in the line of kneeling dead, the sunset blinks out of existence, replaced by a midnight sky illumined only by starlight.

"I'll be damned," he mutters. Calling after the figure: "Say friend, you wouldn't happen to be the priest I've heard so much about? No? No, I didn't think so."

The old man stumbles through the darkness, thick shadows seeming to conspire with the breakdown of his own body to make every step a misery.

He doesn't notice the larger tent until the masked figure comes to a halt before its entrance.

"Watch it, will ya. I may be held together with Scotch tape and string these days but ya don't want to get on the bad side of Ol' Francis."

The acolyte remains silent.

The old man studies the tent; strange geometric patterns unpick themselves from the shadows with the flickering glow from a nearby mesa. The shelter before him consists of several horse blankets draped over large hides thick with matted fur stitched crudely together with skins of a more hairless variety.

"Son of a bitch," Francis drawls in admiration. The acolyte chooses this moment to pull aside one of the hides, revealing an entrance.

Francis mutters "If ya see Kubrick, tell 'em his little stag flick didn't move the pecker once."

Reshouldering the duffel bag the old man crawls carefully inside, issuing a string of painful grunts, before the tent's flap falls shut behind him.

SUE

CHAPTER TWENTY-ONE

OUR FACES ARE OUR FORTUNES

In the days that follow the Dream City Church rally, the coronavirus infection rate soars in Phoenix. The girls now don masks not only before entering stores but also before leaving the house despite temperatures of 105°F or more.

"You're well out of it, ma," I mutter to myself one morning. Though I still struggle to come to terms with how she died and my unwitting part in her death, there is a symmetry to it all that is oddly reassuring. The son I once was is gone now; what mother would want to outlive her child?

As if in reply, I find a lone honeybee struggling along the edge of the pool. More and more it seems Mother Earth and her children are locked in a battle to the death.

Glancing up from the insect I notice for the first time that Hannah has pulled up a chair beside the pool and is now poring over her laptop, her mask dark with perspiration.

Ever since the incident at the store, she's been opening up to me in a way I don't think she dares to with Morgan or Althea. This includes showing me the puffin cam she watches religiously between the school assignments that still trickle in despite the on-again/off-again virus lockdowns.

"How are the puffins today," I ask.

"They're great. But it's like even this has been ruined now."

"You've gone off the puffins?"

"Of course not. I mean I hate it when they get hurt or lose a baby or whatever but I get it, it's nature; I can handle it. It's the people that post messages on the site now that upset me sometimes, that's all."

Peeking over her shoulder I see what's getting her down.

"What's all this?"

"The president's just announced he's going to lift fishing bans around the puffin preserve meaning the puffins could essentially starve. It's not like anyone even asked him to do it. That area's been closed for years— the fishing companies have other places to fish now. But of course he has to get his hands all over everything and ruin it."

"So everyone who watches the puffin cam is upset over this?"

"Well yeah. But there's this woman on here that's like 'I come here to relax, not to hear about politics.' Seriously, that's what she just wrote five minutes ago."

"Nothing's real anymore," I say, squinting against the glare from the pool. "Everything's either a show, a meme, or some other bit of disposable nothing."

"Tell that to the puffins."

The rest of the day I spend in a quiet daze, puttering around Francis' house, moving things around, throwing things out, trying to get comfortable both inside my new skin and inside the wood and stucco nightmare it's been consigned to. Nothing's changing anytime soon. I've got about $20 left to my name.

Some hours later I'm camped out in the old man's bed, staring at silverfish on the ceiling, when the shouting begins outside.

By the time I come outside to see what's going on, Morgan and Althea are on one side of the pool shouting at Hannah on the other.

"Whoah whoah, whoah," I holler over the ruckus. "Suppose we talk about this one at a time? Hannah?"

A snort from Morgan. "Of course you take her side."

"There's a Black Lives Matter protest downtown tonight," Althea interjects. "I'm going and I think these two should come too to show solidarity. End of."

"Not end of," snaps Hannah. "She wants us to go jump in a sea of people, maybe even get thrown in jail, at a time when this city's one big plague pit!"

"Sorry my brothers and sisters are getting slaughtered at such an inconvenient time for you," Althea snaps back.

"We'll still be wearing masks," Morgan adds. "We'll be fine."

"That only keeps us from passing this thing on to other people, it doesn't keep us from getting it," Hannah counters. "Not to mention these masks are like a big red cape to the Trump people." She looks at me for confirmation. "Sue saw it herself at the store the other day."

For the first time in a long while I feel like the grown-up in the room. I can see how things will go if Hannah doesn't accompany them tonight—the schism that will ultimately force her out of the house.

"We're all going," I say. "But only if we promise right here and now that we will have each other's backs out there." Reluctantly, assurances are secured.

Watching them depart, I wonder if Francis has his wolf skin yet. Something scratches at the back of my mind wanting to be let in. Something about hermit crabs and skin-changers, and the destinies that adhere themselves to whatever masks we wear.

FRANCIS

CHAPTER TWENTY-TWO

STATIONS OF THE CROSSED

Inside the tent my eyes are still gettin' used to the lantern light when a fellah on a stool looks up, cockin' his head to one side like he's not quite sure what ta make of me.

"You must be the Bless-me-fadduh hisself," I says. "Pleased ta know ya, friend."

I hold out my shaker fer the customary up and down but the bald, pointy-eared prick just ignores me, busying hisself instead with a stand full of medical instruments.

"What shall I call you," he finally asks.

"Beg pardon? Oh I see—so you *don't* know everything? Well that's a relief. Name's Francis."

That nosferatu head of his pivots in my direction, lantern light flickerin' at me in them small round sunglasses of his. "Well Francis, consider this your exit interview."

"Say again?" My peepers adjusting to the dark, I makes out the rest of his getup now. It's some kinda neck to ankle black leather job, right outa them suck-me-to-hell movies with the little nail-headed fellah.

"Your exit interview." He nods at a seat by his knee. Wrecked by all that walkin' I takes him up on the offer. "You're leaving this life behind.

What I want to know is this: What would you tell mankind if you had the chance?"

"What are you kiddin' me with this?"

"In view of your bloody proclivities, perhaps they have made you feel less than you are?"

"*Less* than I am? Are you havin' me on? My kind are treated like gods! Every day brings a downpour of TV shows and movies and books and I don't know what all, all of it dissectin' people just like me. Brother, this is my *time*!"

"Then why do you seek this change?"

"Look at me! 'For the sword outwears its sheath' and all that jazz. Well this here sheath may be shot all to hell but the sword's as sharp as ever. Just needs a retread job is all."

The Priest considers this for a bit before pinning the bag at my feet. "Is that the 20 thousand?"

"Sure is, friend."

"Well then," he says, pullin' hisself to his feet, "I suppose we should get started."

I follows him back outside, strugglin' to keep up. "Hey fadduh, some of us ain't spring chickens no more?" But this don't slow him none. He climbs a low mesa: up, up, up toward that flickerin' fire. He'll get his, all right, after I gets what I came for.

From the ground the mountain don't seem so high, but the climb takes forever. "So you an actual man-of-the-cloth type, or do they just call you Priest for kicks," I shouts after him.

I'm about to try another approach when he turns to me and says: "How is the girl?"

"Oh ya mean Sue? Aw, she had a bumpy beginnin' but Ol' Francis put her right. Probably got her painted piggies propped up on a chair by my pool even as we speak."

"It will not have gone easy for her," he says, turning back to continue the climb. "The male-female transition is particularly perilous, I find."

"Well hell, it's gotta be easier than the man-wolf shuffle."

"On the contrary, the transition from man to animal is a small matter; a clearing away of the intellect to free the spirit, as simple in its way as the unclogging of a drain. Crossing the gender barrier, however, now that is something else. Think of it as spending a lifetime in a hospital room separated from your fellow patient by a thick curtain. All that time you comfort each other, swapping stories, perhaps sharing hopes concerning your futures."

"And?"

"Now think of that gender transition as a rude pulling away of the curtain, revealing who and what has been on the other side all this time. All the truth that could *not* be communicated so long as you both were separated by gender in this way."

"Never should've tore away the curtain in the first place, if you ask me," I tells him. "Sorry ta interrupt all the navel gazin' but I gotta take me a little siesta." So sayin' I crumple to the ground in slow-mo like a 500-year-old tree in a corporate stroke film.

The Priest regards me for a moment, face unreadable. We can't be more than 50 yards from the source of that flickering glow on the mesa's summit, but this ol' carcass of mine ain't gonna make it no further.

"I knows what yer thinkin', holy man."

"Do you?"

"Ya think all this is about me dodgin' the bullet; makin' a swap afore the wheels fall off."

"Is that what I think?"

"Truth is it's about finally bein' what I was always meant to be. But hell, I'll cop to it: Whoever gets this ol' deathtrap of a body—good luck to 'em, I say. I suppose it's like drivin' yer ol' jalopy into the ground and then sellin' 'er fast to the nearest mark. But I ask you, fadduh, in all honesty, what could be more American than that?"

CHAPTER TWENTY-THREE

THE GIANTS THAT DOG OUR DAYS

Anticipating the evening that lies ahead I try to take a nap but sleep does not come. Staring at Francis' bedroom ceiling, I'm struck by the youthful energy that courses through this new body of mine compared with the older one I left behind just a few weeks ago.

Unable to rest and afraid of spending the remainder of the day agonizing over what's to come, I call Hannah: "How about a hike?"

An hour later we're on the road, now strangely free of the traffic that usually chokes it to a standstill.

"What do you make of all this," I ask, struggling to be heard over the roar of the car's AC and the dampening effects of the face mask.

Hannah shrugs. "It makes me nervous. The virus, the police, this country. But it's also been one thing or another our whole lives, right? So if it wasn't this stuff it'd be some other stuff."

"You don't think it's been a little crazier these last few years?"

"Not really. I think maybe the people back home—you know, DC—I think they're a little more chill in general, but there's always been crazy stuff for as long as I can remember. School shooter drills, security screenings every time you want to go anywhere, a crappy economy pretty much always while everyone's telling you how great it all is, and then people trying to take your money a million different ways online." She laughs. "Getting told several times a week to 'go back to your country.'"

A glance at my reflection in the window reminds me that I may have spent 45 years on this earth, but this new skin belongs to someone much younger; Hannah's looking at me now like a fellow sufferer of 21st century insanity. *Of course* COVID and killer cops and a mad president would seem like just more of the same to someone her age.

As we drive to our hiking destination, we pass the back of an apartment block that appears to hang in the sky, teetering on the edge of a hill as if the backyard has simply been sheared away by a passing meteor.

We turn into the Hilton lot that Francis directed me to not so long ago.

Getting out of the car my eyes briefly alight on an empty cardboard box in the gutter: "In-Car Trash Bag" it reads. This fucking town...

Finding the entrance to the great desert expanse takes me a while, but finally gravel and trees give way to the comforting embrace of empty land. The girl hands me one of the water bottles she's brought for our walk; we both lift our masks just enough to drink.

Stowing the bottles in her sling bag, Hannah heads off without me as if she knows the place better than I.

For a good 20 minutes we roam, marveling at sights strange and beautiful: a car door leaning against a tree, a jack rabbit springing up the mountainside. From a long way off comes the *La Llorona* wail of fire truck sirens instantly joined by the mournful howls of unseen coyotes just beyond the hills. Hannah looks at me, eyes wide with alarm.

"You're not from here, are you," I venture as if I've lived here longer than just a few weeks. Soon our journey takes us to a paved service road curving up and around a steep mountain.

"I'm from DC. Well, Falls Church, Virginia, but nobody knows where that is so I say DC," she confides. "Ever been there?"

I admit that I haven't. At the top of the mountain, our destination, massive water tanks loom.

Hannah stops, eyes glistening behind thick glasses. In them I can see a decision made. Backing away to minimize potential viral exposure, she removes her mask.

"There's this enormous sculpture in Maryland on the waterfront," she says. "More like four or five sculptures, really. A giant head here, an arm there. But when you look at them all together they look like this giant pulling himself out of the ground."

My own mask comes off; I cram it into the pocket of my shorts. "Sounds pretty neat."

"My dad took me to see it once when I was really little but I still remember it. It's always kind of terrified me. When I moved out here for school—I've never told anybody this before—it was mostly because I thought that as long as I'm far away, it can't get me."

Rounding the last bend we peer up at the water silos standing tauntingly out of reach.

"That statue is so huge I guess I assumed it had always been where I first saw it, and always would be. Then last year I discovered it used to be someplace in DC and they just sort of moved it to where I saw it about 10 years ago."

"Weird," I say politely, not sure why she's telling me this.

Hannah's eyes flash angrily. "You don't get it! The giant moved!" She begins to pace. "I know how all this sounds but I feel like this thing has, I don't know, pulled itself out of the ground and is now sort of lumbering its way across the country, leaving a trail of devastation everywhere it goes. And it's getting closer all the time. I mean look at some of the places just a few miles from where it's 'resting'; houses that aren't much more than a pile of bricks with aluminum siding thrown over them, smashed up cars with no tires. And now all this stuff that's happening around us..."

Suddenly I remember Goya's painting of the Colossus, its back turned to some small town nestled in a valley not unlike this one. I think of the apartment block we so recently passed whose backyard looked as if it had been shorn away, and picture a giant clumsily making this happen on its slow lurch toward...where?

"We are living in the wake of this invisible *thing* as it crashes through our lives and no one seems to notice," Hannah says. "I mean yeah, we all get that something's very wrong, but people keep saying it's politics or there's no money or there's wars or everyone's sick, or things just aren't as good as they used to be...but none of it really seems to express this, this..."

"Dread?"

The word lingers between us for a moment. Then we slip our masks back on and continue the long trudge up the mountainside. At last we arrive at the water tower fence.

Suddenly I realize I've been here before. I turn and see the Dream City Church standing stark and white in the distance. Turning back I find Hannah's eyes are not on the vista but rather the sloping valley below, its boulders, rocks and desert brush giving the impression of a volcanic spiral of lava cooled and set all the way down.

"We did Dante's *Inferno* in high school," she says, peering down into the chasm. "In it Lucifer was enormous. And when he fell from heaven, he did so head first. Down. Down. Down...into the center of the earth. And his enormous body just sort of remained there, upside down."

Giants on our heels, the devil at our feet, and an unseen pestilence waiting to plow us all under, while the Dream City Church sits patiently by, glistening in the morning sun.

CHAPTER TWENTY-FOUR

THE PASSION OF ST. FRANCIS

We're maybe 50 feet from the top of the mountain afore I sees the source of that flickerin': a tremendous fire, its center a small house ringed round by an iron fence, spear tips angled outward. Through the flames I can just makes out large rocks and rubble, something I seen back in Phoenix with Sue only a few weeks ago.

"What the fuzzy walnuts you playin' at," I sputter, face boilin' with the fire.

The Priest gives me this little smile. "I'm sure you're familiar with the creation myth," he says. "In the beginning there was an enormous explosion, expelling all the material of our universe outward, elements sent to swirl about in great clouds. It was only in the settling of that dust that the planets formed, and the stars. And man."

"Yes well that's jim-dandy and all, but what's that got ta do with me?"

"We now find ourselves in the middle of a second Big Bang. And this swapping of skins, these transformations—they are all one small part of it."

"I didn't come all this way for the chakra-pocky ya been doling out tonight!" I drops the bag at his feet. "There's yer money. Now suppose you gimme what I came for." Much as I try to appear menacing, my peepers get drawn back to the burning pile of bricks and stone.

He laughs. "Very well. Get it out, then," he says, nudging the bag with a bare foot. "Every last note."

Gettin' as close as I dare to the burnin' ruins, I catch sight of bits of currency blackening in the embers inside the fence.

Suddenly this low wailin' tickles my ears from the other side of the fire. Half fallin', half shufflin', I goes round to find its source.

When I finally spot 'em, there are 6 or 7 bodies lyin' on the ground. A couple are shoved right up against them iron bars, the scalding metal sinkin' right into the girl's cheek like a hot knife into butter. The guy's slumped over next to her, forehead sizzlin' like pork fat against another part of the fence. The rest of them bodies are just dark mounds, all in various stages of collapse, down the back of the mountainside. Dead, smoldering piles against black earth.

Turnin' my attention back to the couple I get the crawlies. Young in the face but old in the flesh, both of 'em—middle-age abortions that've seen it all. Like the cores of their being have been carved out, left to crackle in the fire.

The fire.

"Mary mothera Jesus…"

I see it now. The girl's got one hand thrust through them bars, fist no more than a bubblin' knot of flesh round a hunk of glowin' ash. Once legal tender, now just tinder.

Noddin' at the pair I say: "Livin' proof of yer 'no refunds' policy, are they?"

"Rebirth is a two-part process," he says. "The first is simple enough: shedding the old skin, leaving behind the shell that's come to feel like a prison. But the second step? That's where the challenge truly begins."

"What challenge? New skin, new life, ain't it?"

"Once they're finally free of their prisons of flesh—why would they want to take on another?"

"Maybe these wretches lost their guts along the way, whatdoIknow? But there's no goin' back fer me!" This last bit I spits into his smug little face, chuckin' my cash through the bars and into the flames. I can still see flecks of ol' Mary's blood on the corner of one of them bills as it curls into char.

"Very well," says the Priest, wavin' a claw-like hand at something large and loping comin' up the mountain in our direction. "St. Francis, I welcome you to your Gubbio."

For one brief moment all I can makes out is the robes of the silent monk that brought me here knotted round the legs of a wolf-like beast, the frayed fabric dragged through the dust behind it. Like a soul makin' good its escape.

SUE

CHAPTER TWENTY-FIVE

THE DESERT WAITS

Standing in one sock and an old Diamondbacks tee, I marvel at myself in Francis' bathroom mirror. Not only do I have to dress for what is shaping up to be a boiling hot Phoenix day, I also have to keep in mind things I've never in my life had to consider before: police abuse, the virus, the violent unpredictability of crowds.

I text Hannah: "I don't know if I can do this."

There's a feeling in the air, an oppressive sense of doom. Last night's horrible dreams only make it worse.

"There are huge parts of the body-swap experience that I think I've just blocked out," I admitted to Clarissa when she phoned me a couple days ago. "It's like they only come out in my dreams."

"Yeah, that's pretty much how it went for me, too," Clarissa said. "It's been almost two months now and I'm still discovering new things about my time in the desert."

"You actually *remember* it?"

"It's strange. It's like the Priest buries himself inside your head and kind of feeds you the memories you need as you need them. It reminds me a lot of when I taught myself to read tarot cards as a kid. Just this feeling that the cards of my life are getting turned over for me one at a time. It started in my dreams but lately I've been experiencing it when I'm awake, too."

A few hours later Morgan, Althea, Hannah and I are all jammed inside Hannah's car, slowly creeping down 7th Avenue toward downtown, the AC doing little to mitigate the stifling effects of our face masks.

If I'd been expecting some kind of St. Crispin's Day speech when we finally arrived at our destination, I was rudely disappointed.

"It's good you're here," Althea tells us as we finish stowing water bottles in our backpacks. "But remember, this is about Black lives, OK? It's *our* lives on the line so it's Black people that have to call the shots."

Other than exchanging a brief look with Hannah, I say nothing, but can't help thinking: 'Even now, in this new skin, in this horrible shit hole of a city where everything is falling apart all around us, it's still "us" and "them" bitchy little notes chucked back and forth over the walls of our skins.'

Walls.

The word is still haunting me 20 minutes later when we finally prepare to join the other protesters.

"Something you wanna say," Althea asks. Hannah and Morgan exchange nervous looks.

I take a deep breath: "I get the importance of all this, the whole Black Lives Matter movement."

"But?"

"No buts. It's just that it's like we've been walled off from each other so long, we've forgotten how to just be around other people. The minute anyone puts their head up and asks a question or ventures a thought—it's 'get back in your box, bitch. Don't question me, you don't know what it's like.'"

Althea is about to respond when she's cut off by a slow clap.

"For all of us who get told off 20,000 times a day on Twitter for daring to say anything about anything," says Hannah, "thank you."

Morgan looks around uncomfortably as if waiting to see which way the wind will blow.

"Look," I say, "this isn't about you or me; it's about where we're all headed."

What I'm about to tell her I've never told anyone before because it's a memory that hasn't surfaced until this very moment.

"When I was a kid my mom and I went to Ireland to visit family. Things were really bad then between Northern Ireland and the rest of the country. Her cousin lived in Belfast—one of the toughest places to be during 'the troubles.'

"So we're on the Catholic side of the street and we can't even see the Protestant side because they've put up this enormous wall right down the middle. 'Peace walls,' they called them, I think. So one night we sneak over to the other side of the wall."

Morgan looks around nervously at the protesters continuing to fill the streets. I raise my voice over the noise.

"All along the Protestant side of the wall was graffiti, the most hateful things I've ever seen written in a public place. The hate in those words, in the illustrations—all of it directed at Catholics like my family. They didn't know us at all, but our very existence seemed to offend them somehow. They wanted us dead."

Althea shakes her head. "It's not the same," she says. And that's it. Hannah and Morgan go back to preparing for what's to come, occasionally peeling back a mask to reveal a sweaty face sucking down air.

It's not the masks suffocating us, is all I can think. *It's the whole fucking way we've sandbagged ourselves off from each other as if getting ready for a hurricane of our own making. One "peace wall" at a time.*

Downtown, half a dozen city blocks teem with banners, signs, backpacks and bandanas, a solid mile of skins black, brown and white glistening in the sun.

Ditching Hannah's car, we allow ourselves to be carried down toward the heart of the city in a river of bodies crushed tightly together, virus be damned.

"It's insane to protest deadly practices and then go around potentially exposing people to an illness that can kill them dead," Hannah snaps after I suggest removing our own masks.

Before long Althea breaks away to join another group of friends jammed together behind a banner proclaiming their Black pride and strength. Morgan, too, disappears, having spotted a guy from one of her classes. "He's probably the main reason she's here," Hannah shouts over the din. "She's been dying for an excuse to hang out with him for months now."

Suddenly I sense another presence: Phoenix's finest amassing in great numbers in an alley across the street, afternoon sun glinting off dirt caked shields.

"Dying for an excuse," I mutter, feeling the rude snap of a Tarot card being turned over in the back of my mind. A lesson from the desert returns to sear the retinas of my memory.

"This isn't right," I say, my words lost in the roar of the crowd. "We've gotta get out of here!" Grabbing Hannah's arm, I lead her through the crush.

"Where are we going?"

"We need to find higher ground!"

Despite my mask a thin layer of dust coats the back of my throat, borne there on the hot winds of a memory once lost, now found.

Higher ground.

The men in black flack jackets and helmets surge forward. Grabbing my arm, Hannah drags me through the crowd and into a back alley where she breaks into a run. "This way!"

I follow her around a building and back into the crush, barely conscious of my surroundings as we cross the main thoroughfare.

This is blocked off by even more cops, and other men in black whose uniforms don't quite match, even if their AR-15s do.

Only a few seconds pass between the time we slip into the back entrance of a dilapidated residential hotel and the first volley of screams that erupt somewhere a block away.

"It's OK," Hannah explains. "I run errands for a disabled guy who lives here." She dangles a swipe badge from a frayed black lanyard.

"Can you get us to the roof?"

In a few minutes that's where we find ourselves, clinging to each other despite the heat. Down below, the roiling masses start to crumble beneath a steady rain of black truncheons.

Memories from weeks ago, hopelessly jumbled, come rushing back now. How I ended up climbing the mesa opposite the burning ruins back in the desert, I can't say. All I know is that it happened after my transformation.

I was still lurching precariously around on limbs that, though decades younger, seemed spindly compared to the muscular male appendages I'd been used to before. All I'd known for sure that morning was that a great deluge was coming, and it would wash me and everything else away if I didn't find higher ground fast.

Cresting the summit of the low mesa I'd seen them then.

There were maybe a dozen, naked and evenly spaced along the summit. All seemed to be facing different directions, some with heads bowed, others with their faces raised to the breaking dawn. All had arms splayed at 45 degree angles from their sides, their eyes empty sockets.

Empty skins freed from their owners. Yet still standing.

Once free of their current prisons of the flesh, who truly would want to take on another?

I'd stumbled up the rocky incline until I, too, reached the top. From face to empty face I ricocheted, spinning round on uncertain feet until I happened upon one skin in particular. It was the naked hide of an old man, patches of gray hair glistening in the morning sun. Reluctantly, I followed his gaze down into the valley below. And dropped to my knees. Though I didn't hear the Priest behind me, I knew he was there.

"You're like some kind of perverted exorcist," I hissed at him, my eyes never leaving the valley. "Instead of driving out the demons, you drive out the souls of human beings instead."

From the moment I'd first come into the dark cleric's presence, I'd felt a wellspring of terror inside. Only now, the sight that stretched out before me had replaced that fear with a larger emotion, more profound: hopelessness.

Stretching out down below in every direction were stationary figures of every description. All, I knew instinctively, were as empty as those around me atop the mesa.

From behind I could feel the Priest's approach. "Listen well," he said. "This earth is choked with empty vessels, there for the filling by whatever low creatures would debase themselves by entering them."

As he spoke, my mind began to fill with shocking images: sperm and egg, the yin-yang flows of separate streams only occasionally touching before spinning off into the wider world.

Now, this moment, peering down at the masses in the Phoenix streets below, protesters and police, I see it all at last, what the Priest had meant.

"Why are they doing this?!" Hannah shouts above the chaos.

Laughing, I remove my face mask, holding it out over the city before allowing the hot breeze to snatch it from my fingertips. Out it sails over the mad city below.

"There's nothing *in* them at all anymore," I tell her gently. "Just empty skins. After years spent driving away every thought and feeling with phones and music and booze and God only knows what else. Now they're little more than laundry hung out to dry, snapping in a breeze they cannot see."

"So that's it," Hannah asks angrily.

"What do you want me to say? *There's* your giant. They're crashing around down there like free radicals in the bloodstream, tearing off bits of the planet as they go. However much you want them to pull themselves together and take responsibility for their actions, they are incapable of doing it. You might as well yell at the rain."

"Then you're just going to give them all a pass? They're not responsible so let them do their worst?"

With a touch as light as a lover's, I remove the mask from her face and let it follow my own down, down, down into the churning flesh below.

"The desert waits for me as it waits for you," I tell her, "and for the rest of this sorry, hollow armada. It waits for us to sail off in one direction, course correct, bob for years in our own Sargasso Sea, before continuing on toward our inevitable destination. Sooner or later everything flows into its valleys and turns to dust."

Somewhere above the wail of police sirens and the roar of the mob, I hear it—the lumbering footfalls of Hannah's giant closing in.

"And, when the desert truly wants to punish us, it grants us our heart's desire."

Farther off in the distance, the frustrated howl of a wolf builds long and low in a throat choked with dust. The sound of a beast loping off in search of its first prey, only to find there is nothing left to hunt.

www.ingramcontent.com/pod-product-compliance
Ingram Content Group UK Ltd.
Pitfield, Milton Keynes, MK11 3LW, UK
UKHW061223180426
11947UKWH00027B/1997